THE BOTTOM

Other Novels by Howard Owen

Littlejohn

Fat Lightning

Answers to Lucky

The Measured Man

Harry & Ruth

The Rail

Turn Signal

Rock of Ages

The Reckoning

Oregon Hill

The Philadelphia Quarry

Parker Field

A WILLIE BLACK MYSTERY

THE BOTTOM

HOWARD OWEN

THE PERMANENT PRESS
Sag Harbor, NY 11963

For information, address:
The Permanent Press
4170 Noyac Road
Sag Harbor, NY 11963
www.thepermanentpress.com

Library of Congress Cataloging-in-Publication Data

Owen, Howard—
The bottom / by Howard Owen.
pages ; cm
ISBN 978-1-57962-392-0
I. Title.

PS3565.W552B68 2015
813'.54—dc23 2015013684

Printed in the United States of America

As always, to Karen

CHAPTER ONE

Thursday, September 12, 2013

Main Street Station doesn't get used much, at least not by Amtrak passengers. You can see it, in its neglected splendor, when you're driving through Richmond on—God help you—I-95. It's more symbolic than anything else, a reminder that we once gave a damn about rail service and could afford public buildings you could brag about. A couple of trains coming from Newport News headed north, a couple more going back—most days, that's it. All the rest of the traffic goes through a station out in the suburbs that reminds me of a Greyhound terminal. In a city that has not one but two drop-dead gorgeous passenger depots, one of them has been turned into a science museum and the other, the one I'm standing in here, doesn't have enough traffic to keep dogs from sleeping on the tracks.

The last train got in at six thirty last night, give or take an hour or two, but what are the odds that one of the passengers was hanging out in the little side room where they discovered her? Even if he had seen the kid all bundled up in a bedroll, he might have figured she was just one more tired-ass runaway looking for a place to sleep.

Somebody finally found her about eight forty-five this morning. A family, headed up to New York City, wandered into the little room. The father said he tried to rouse the girl inside the bedroll and then realized she was dead.

NOBODY IN THE newsroom ever seems the least bit concerned that I don't get to sleep until sometime after two, and that's on nights when I don't heed the siren song of Penny Lane Pub or some lonely staffer who has a bottle too big for one person to finish alone.

Last night being a Wednesday, and me trying to be a better person these days, I'd had probably seven hours of shut-eye—almost enough—when Sally Velez gave me my wake-up call.

"You sound like you just got out of bed," she said.

I told her I had to get out of bed to answer the goddamned phone.

"Well," she said, "as long as you're up, you might as well get dressed. Looks like that creep has struck again."

OK. She had my attention. I didn't have to ask which creep.

"Where?"

"The train station."

"Which one?"

"Main Street."

"Tweety Bird?"

"Yeah."

I told her I'd be there in twenty minutes, which was optimistic. Later when I'm fully awake, I'll thank Sally, who could have gone to Baer or another pup, any of whom would love to do this one. Sally and I have some history, and she knows I've been on this story from the start, since the first girl's body showed up. Because I'm night cops and sin loves the dark, I have been involved from the beginning. One runaway or homeless girl turns up dead in our fair city and it rates B1, especially if she's white. Another one ups the ante to A1, whatever the victim's color, especially if the needle points to "serial killer." A third one and you see a noticeable rise in the sale of guns and pepper spray. And now it looks like we have four of a kind, a hot hand if you're trying to sell newspapers. And we are always—with middling results—trying to sell newspapers.

Well, some of us are trying harder than others. The big dogs, the ones who still get bonuses, mostly for laying people off, definitely want to see better sales. I just want to get a story and sink my teeth into it like a pit bull with anger issues. Sometimes that results in a few papers being bought and read, putting me, if only briefly, on the same page with the suits. This harmonic convergence usually doesn't last long.

This one, though, makes me lose that much-hyped journalistic objectivity. It pisses me off.

They had already removed the body by the time I got here. I'm able to persuade Gillespie, one of the few cops who actually speak to me these days, to tell me what he knows.

He says the girl didn't look like she was any more than fourteen or fifteen. He said that, when they unzipped the bag so they could see something other than the top of her head, they saw that she had been strangled. Gillespie said he wasn't sure, but that it looked like she'd been "messed with." It's almost charming to hear the fat, sweating Gillespie pull his punches. He means she probably was raped. Why not? The other three were, multiple times and in various orifices. All the animals around here aren't in the Maymont Park zoo.

"Her hair was all dirty and matted," he says. "She couldn't have weighed more than ninety pounds. Probably hadn't eaten in a week."

Having been a sort of underdog myself, I really hate this shit. Growing up on the Hill, you had bullies who terrorized anybody or anything smaller or weaker than they were. I probably got in more fights butting into other people's problems along those lines than I did trying to take care of my own self.

Plus I think about Andi, who ran away a couple of times when she was playing troubled teen, before I did much to honor the title of father. That could have been her lying on a couch in a waiting room at Main Street Station, waiting half a day or so for somebody to know she's dead.

"When they catch the son of a bitch," Gillespie says, "I hope they'll let me come watch when they pull the switch."

Actually, they use lethal injection now, I remind my fat, flat-footed friend, but I'd like to be there with you.

We're standing in a corner of the huge station. There's nobody here except a dozen or so cops and me, although the TV stations soon will come baying like deranged beagles. The only thing that keeps print journalists from shame sometimes is the knowledge that, no matter how mindlessly we might exploit other people's suffering, TV will not be outdone. Right after the second body turned up, one of the local stations starting dubbing the killer the Vampire Slayer. Its lack of originality was topped only by its inaccuracy. The first girl lost a lot of blood, but there was never any sign that Dracula had been reincarnated in Richmond. One of the other stations did what they called a reenactment of the murder, supposedly to show young women how to fend off psychopaths. In the reenactment, the victim wins. If only.

Chief Jones arrives with great flourish. I swear to God, he now has his own bodyguard, at city expense. Supposedly he heard that the mayor had a full staff of goons to protect him from the taxpayers and thought he ought to have at least one. And people wonder why city taxes are so high.

I'm not officially, or unofficially, supposed to be here. Gillespie didn't want to let me in, but I persuaded him to relent, pointing out that my next epistle to the readers won't hit the streets for about twenty hours. The chief is not of such a charitable nature. He's probably feeling some warmth on his backside as the fourth victim takes her place at the city morgue. The chief is pretty insistent that I leave, making his feelings known in a voice that makes me glad I don't have a hangover.

"Chill, L.D.," I tell him. "I'm not even on the clock. Just a concerned citizen."

My using his first name, instead of eliciting some bonhomie from those long-ago days when we would have a beer or two or shoot some hoops, just seems to make him madder. Most of the recent history Larry Doby Jones and I share might not give the chief a warm, fuzzy feeling. He has been known to ride a bad arrest all the way to the bottom. I have been known to point this out in our newspaper. I'm afraid there is a chill in our relationship.

He has another cop escort me from the station as the bodyguard glowers. I look back to see him searing Gillespie's pink ears. My name, I fear, is being taken in vain.

BACK AT THE paper, I stop by Sally's desk and thank her for thinking of me. She grunts her acknowledgment.

Nothing much is happening yet in the newsroom. It's so quiet I have trouble concentrating. Even in the late afternoon, with deadlines approaching, things are a lot quieter than they used to be. The surviving reporters and editors occupy only a fraction of what once was a humming, mildly competitive daily newspaper. We are bunched together, much as a herd of zebras might close ranks as the lions close in. This time of the morning, though, the only place quieter than this probably is the Main Street Station.

"Same kind of shit?" Sally asks.

"Looks like it. Strangulation. Seems to be a runaway, at least according to Gillespie. No identification."

"Raped?"

"Probably."

"God damn it."

"Yeah."

I dash off a few paragraphs for our readers in the ether, who seem strangely resistant to pay for what we've been giving them for free since before some of them learned to read. We do have a "pay wall" now, which means we give you an appetizer and then charge a little if you go for the full, five-course meal. Sadly many of our readers seem more than happy to just nosh a little and move on. They can't keep themselves from wasting money on porn sites and anything Amazon sells, but when it comes to the local news, their self-restraint is remarkable. My suggestion that we join 'em and start running beaver shots on Page 2 has so far been rebuffed.

I leave, fully awake now but not getting paid for another five hours or so. I'll write the story for the print edition when I come in officially. I'll even read that one first before I send it.

The day's first Camel jump-starts my brain cells. I ought to go back and take a nap. My roomie, Custalow, should be at work by now. He's the hired help, striving to make the Prestwould where we live even more worthy of its four-digit monthly condo fee.

But I'm curious. Very curious, it has been suggested. I want to know just how the hell a dead girl gets transported into even a train station as sleepy as this one without anyone noticing.

I am right in assuming that, by the time I get back, the police will be gone. I also am right in assuming that they haven't yet interviewed the guard who was supposed to be on duty from noon to nine P.M. yesterday. When I walk into the lobby, a young, overweight black guy is standing by his desk. It looks like a couple of his buddies are keeping him company, probably wanting to share this moment of gruesome excitement in what otherwise must be the world's most boring job.

His name badge says "Williams," so I call him Mr. Williams, even though he's about half my age. I tell him I have a few more questions about the dead body that somehow materialized just outside the lobby, on his watch. I somehow forget to mention that I'm asking on behalf of our shrinking readership rather than the police.

Mr. Williams's buddies move away a little. They, like him, must be under the mistaken impression that I'm a cop.

"Later, JoJo," one of them calls.

I ask JoJo, with whom I now assume a first-name familiarity, if he can remember anything unusual that might have happened during his shift yesterday.

"Man" he says, "I didn't know nothing—anything—about any of this until Cheryl called me this morning. I swear I didn't see anything."

I ask JoJo if he might have taken a break or two during the evening.

"Thass allowed," he says. "They let you take bathroom breaks and such."

I note that, if I had his job, with all this excitement—a train coming through every six hours or so—I might be tempted to slip out for maybe half an hour or so.

"You can't prove that," he says, frowning.

"Well, if we can pinpoint time of death, maybe we can do something with that. Say the coroner says it was, oh, 9:37 P.M. And we start asking you how it was that somebody could take somebody into that side room, strangle her and leave while you were taking a piss. How long does it take you to take a piss, JoJo?"

This is all bullshit. I'm betting JoJo doesn't know yet that the girl probably was already dead when the bastard dumped her in here. No signs of muss or fuss. Just a quiet little body, asleep forever in her bedroll.

JoJo is thinking, probably about how he can give the police—of which he believes I am one, for some reason—enough information to get me off his back and still save his job. It won't be easy, especially if JoJo is on the same Einstein level as the part-time VCU students we usually pay to "guard" the Prestwould.

"OK," he says, palms out, "it's like this. I got a call. It was this girl, sweet-sounding thing. She said she was a bartender over at Havana 59, and that a guy just left her twenty dollars and my phone number. She knew my name and everything.

Told her he was my friend, she said, and wanted to treat me to a couple of drinks. But I had to come over right then."

"So you went."

"Hey, there wasn't anything going on here, man. It was dead as it is right now."

"What time?"

"It was after nine. I went over, and the bartender, same one I talked to, she said the guy had left the money for me, said the drinks were on him. I swear, I wasn't gone but half an hour."

I figure it took JoJo more than half an hour to drink up that twenty dollars of mojitos. When pressed, he says he's sure he was back by ten. And, no, he doesn't remember the girl's name.

He describes her. White girl, blonde hair, kind of long face. And, oh yeah, a tattoo on the back of her right hand. It was a Washington Redskins logo.

There are plenty of bartender-waitresses in Richmond with blonde hair. Many have long faces, no doubt. But the only one I know of who has both those attributes and a Redskins logo imbedded, for some damned reason, on the back of her right hand is my daughter.

I thank JoJo, who doesn't thank me back. I tell him I'm sure there will be more questions, which doesn't seem to make him happy.

As I am leaving the station, I see what is obviously a plainclothes car pulling up to conduct the interview JoJo thinks already has been conducted. The chief will no doubt drop his opinion of me to the subfreezing level when the cops find out I've already interviewed the guard and let him think I was one of our city's finest. Well, I don't think there's a crime against keeping your mouth shut.

Andi is still working, despite being three months pregnant. She's not showing enough to notice yet. And, when I call her, she says that she is, indeed, working at Havana 59, has been for the past two months. I probably should have known that, but it's hard to keep track. Andi's worked at a couple of dozen places around town since she started her long march toward what I fervently hope is a college degree. She and Thomas Jefferson Blandford V are not married, nor do they intend to be, it seems. That, Andi says, is her call.

Oh, yes. Andi is living with my mother, who can tell her all she needs to know about the joys of single parenthood.

She has to leave for work in an hour. I tell her not to leave until I get there.

"Is this important?" she says. "I can't afford to be late again."

I assure her it is, indeed, important.

I HAVE TIME to run by Peggy's before Andi and I both go on the clock.

Peggy's seen better days. It's been more than a year since the one decent male companion she's had in the last half-century left us. Les Hacker, God bless him, kept my dope-addled mom in the general vicinity of happiness for a long time. It is her regret and mine that she never really had time to pay him back. He already was sinking into dementia when one of my nuttier Prestwould neighbors shot him and put him on the fast track to whatever reward awaits a man who put everybody before himself. I have no doubt that, if Finlay Rand hadn't shot Les, Peggy would have taken care of him, without ever giving it a damned thought, until he'd soiled his last adult diaper. Rand, I'm happy to say, is still alive in a prison hospital, paralyzed but not brain-damaged enough not to know how much better he'd be dead, if somebody cared enough to pull the plug.

"I didn't know," Peggy said at the funeral, "that there were men like Les Hacker until I met him."

Without Les, Peggy is pretty much dependent on (a) weed and (b) Awesome Dude. I'm not sure which is the least beneficial to her. I kid Peggy that we should be looking for a retirement home for her in Colorado, where she will never have to worry about being busted, but I'm pretty sure no cop working Oregon Hill is going to try to bust Peggy Black for the ounce or so she keeps around the house. She's probably already baked whatever brain cells the evil weed can take from her, so what's the harm?

Awesome lives in her English basement when it's too cold to hang out in his natural habitat, the great outdoors. Awesome is getting older, and the temperature at which he prefers to take his butt indoors at night seems to have risen a bit. He's certainly not much help. Peggy has to depend on me and some of my old Hill buddies to fix the roof when it leaks or to work on her car, because no one in his right mind would put Awesome on a ladder or let him mess with any kind of machinery. Still he doesn't do any harm as long as he doesn't burn down the house. He uses some of his disability money to help with the rent and the dope.

It surprised me when Andi moved in. It seems that the idea of fatherhood took some of the romance out of the relationship from Mr. Blandford's perspective. Andi said he did offer to marry her, much in the same sense as the guy who smashes into your car offers to pay for damages. Not, in other words, with a glad heart.

"It turns out he was an asshole," was Andi's assessment. I never met the father of my percolating grandchild, but I'm willing to accept Andi's evaluation. I kind of wish he'd been a little more of one, so I could kick the shit out of him or at least have the satisfaction of having tried.

Andi has been a godsend, I must admit. She's the daughter Peggy never had, and Andi seems to find Peggy more amusing that I did when I was her age. Maybe sense of humor skips a generation, or maybe it's just less embarrassing to have your grandmother leave the house wearing unmatched shoes than it is when it's your mother.

When Andi moved in, Peggy had pretty much retreated to her own private emotional cave. Even Awesome Dude noticed it.

"Dude," he said, when he called me a couple of months ago, "Peggy just ain't her old self. She doesn't even stay high but about half the time."

My mother's average high-ness is still below her traditional level. She worries about second-hand smoke. Can't have her first great-grandchild popping out with a case of the munchies. But her mood has perked up considerably. Maybe it really does take a village, like Hillary said, and this one even has, in Mr. Dude, its own village idiot.

I kiss Peggy and then take Andi to the kitchen, where we can talk. With me out of the living room, I can hear Peggy switch the channel back to Fox News, which I have assured her will rot her brain faster than pot ever could. The idea that my grandchild might be absorbing anything at all from Rush Limbaugh is hard to endure. Andi always gets her to switch to something more edifying, like *Duck Dynasty*, when she's in the room.

I tell Andi about the call. She confirms that she made it.

"Omigod," she says. "That black guy was from the train station? And he was supposed to be there when that girl was killed?"

"When she was dumped, anyhow. What about the other guy? The one who gave you the twenty."

"I don't know."

"What did he look like?"

Andi shakes her head.

"I never saw him."

How, I ask my flesh and blood, can that be?

"I got this call, on my cell. The guy said there was an envelope under the napkin at the bar. I looked, and there was a napkin somebody had taken from a table and set there. There were two twenties and a note. The guy said one twenty was for me and the other one was for drinks for this guy

I was supposed to call. Said he was an old friend. The message was on a piece of paper. Which, no, I don't have. I threw it away."

Mr. Williams was more than glad to slip away from his boring job and have a drink or two on somebody else's dime.

"He asked me who was treating him, but, like I said, I don't know."

I tell her that the cops probably will be asking her the same questions sometime soon.

"Shit," Andi says. "I'll probably lose my job."

None of this is your fault, I assure her after encouraging her to see if she can dredge up anything from her memory.

"That's not it," she says, wiping away a tear. "We're supposed to share our tips."

I tell her that the twenty somebody slipped her to ensure that JoJo Williams would abandon his post for a while probably doesn't qualify as a tip.

"Besides," I add, "there are plenty of places that would hire you in a minute."

Hell, most of them already have, at least once.

CHAPTER TWO

Friday

Four murders in eighteen months are definitely enough to light a fire under our plucky chief of police and his minions. Chains are being yanked.

JoJo Williams, who no doubt is already out of a job, talked to the real police and told them more or less the same story he told me. When the detective who interviewed JoJo found out that the guard thought he'd already talked with the cops, I am told by Peachy Love—my eyes and ears in the world of law enforcement—Chief Jones took my name in vain again. Lucky guess. He'd like to nail me for obstruction of justice or felony pain-in-the-ass, but there's no law I know of against interviewing potential witnesses. How was I to know that JoJo would think I was cop? I am so misunderstood.

And they've already interviewed Andi, who also told them what she told me. What she didn't tell them, per my instructions, is that she's my daughter. A wise officer might have wondered, but I guess Black's a fairly common name. It'll get out eventually, but, as I told my daughter, there's no sense in just giving information away. Let 'em work for it. It'll be good for them.

And so the city is in lockdown mode. Making it more worrisome is that there isn't any particular element that can wipe its brow and say, "Thank God that couldn't happen here." The killer has been rather democratic.

The first one was found lying in the dirt at Texas Beach, back in March of 2012. Her body had been thrown into some bushes. Nobody but the homeless goes down to the river that time of year, and she'd been dead a couple of days before they found her.

Her name was Kelli Jonas. She was a twenty-year-old white girl who had gotten an associate's degree in dental hygiene and had just started working for a dentist in the West End.

The night she disappeared, she had been underage drinking with some friends at a bar on West Main, and her friends said she left by herself. She never made it home, or at least she never got as far as unlocking her front door. Her keys were still in the purse they found floating in a little pool of water at the river's edge.

When they found her, she had been raped, and she had definitely been murdered. Her throat was cut. She had bled to death there beside the James. It appeared that she had several stab wounds before she was allowed to die. She'd been bound and gagged, but, that time of year, it's doubtful that anyone could have heard her even if she'd been allowed to scream.

For a while it was big news. She came from a solid middle-class family out in Henrico, and white and middle class will always get you better play in our paper than poor and black. About the only clue the cops could dredge up was some partially obscured boot prints. They never even found the knife.

Then we, and our readers, got distracted with other things, as we often do, and Kelli Jonas got consigned to that nether world where the cops are still trying, kind of, and we come back once a year and do an update, reopening the family's wounds for no good purpose.

The second one showed up six months later, in September. Chanelle Williams was a seventeen-year-old girl from the

East End. She stopped going to school when she was fifteen and was involved with some people who seemed to think her best career choices were either prostitute or drug runner.

Whoever did it dumped her much abused body in the Kanawha Canal, or rather in one of the boats that take tourists along our belated attempt to—like every other city in America with a river, creek or sewage lagoon—emulate San Antonio's River Walk. One of the workmen found it the next morning. As with Kelli Jonas, she'd been dead for at least a day.

She wasn't in very good shape. For a while, it was assumed that she had been done in by one of her felonious mentors. And, being African American, the dudgeon level didn't run quite so high, at least among white Richmonders.

But then one of the cops noticed the tattoo. It was on her right ankle, not more than three inches high. It appeared to have been done in the last day or two, but that wasn't the big news. The big news was that it was a Tweety Bird, like in the old cartoons. It was the same tattoo, in the same place, as the one they found on Kelli Jonas.

After the police determined, to the best of their limited capacities, that none of the characters connected to Chanelle Williams had any link to Kelli Jonas, they, our newspaper and the rest of the town came to the conclusion that we had a nondiscriminatory, psychopathic nut on our hands.

Young women loaded up on Mace and traveled in packs. But eventually, you get careless, and the young do believe they will live for damn ever. Every time I'd confront Andi with the hard, cold fact that somebody had raped, butchered and murdered two girls her age, she would assure me she could take care of herself.

The third one occurred almost exactly a year after the first one and six months after the second one, back in March. This time the body was found at the entrance to the Church Hill tunnel. Everybody who grew up in Richmond or has lived there any time at all knows about the tunnel. For some reason, the C&O built a train tunnel under Church Hill after the Civil War. One day in 1925, it collapsed, burying four workers, a locomotive and some flat cars. Neither the train nor the workers have been recovered or ever will be. They are sealed forever beneath one of the city's most historic neighborhoods, somewhere below where Patrick Henry gave his "Give me liberty or give me death" speech.

Lorrie Estrada might not have appreciated the history, even if she was still alive when she was brought there to die. She was a third-year student at VCU. She'd grown up in Fairfax County and was in some sort of high-tech premed major that seemed to assure her future success.

Her parents and her friends said she didn't drink, and she didn't date very often. The last time anyone saw her, she was between her apartment on Grove and the VCU library.

She had the Tweety Bird tattoo. She had the same kind of damage as the other two. This time the danger alert went up and it stayed up. Even now, six months later, even before the fourth victim showed up in the Main Street Station anteroom, there is a sense of fear. Just two months ago, a female student at Virginia Union shot a guy in the leg because she thought he was stalking her. Turns out he was just walking the same route as she was, but you can't be too careful.

There are barely 200,000 people living in the city, hub of a metropolitan area of about 1.3 million. When three young women die horribly at the hands of the same unknown stranger in the space of a year, it seems like a very small place. You start seeing demons everywhere.

And now there are four.

Jessica Caldwell was just fourteen years old. She had run away from home the week before, and her parents hadn't been able to arouse much interest in finding her. Despite her mother's tearful declaration that she was a good girl, she had had some problems, mostly with drugs and rebellion. She might have turned up in some shelter, been reclaimed by her parents and gone on to live a long happy life. Instead she is the latest trophy in some murdering bastard's game.

REJUVENATED BY A good night's sleep, a tasty lunch of leftover meatloaf and my two-Camel walk to the paper, I'm in the newsroom by two, reading this morning's breathless headline: Tweety Bird Killer strikes again. They had to cut a couple of grafs to make it fit. No problem. I'll just work them into tomorrow's story. I have a feeling I'll be writing this one for a while.

Wheelie comes up behind me.

"How's it going? Anything new?"

"Not much. The cops are crapping themselves. They still don't have a clue."

"This guy must be pretty good."

"Yeah. Practice makes perfect."

Wheelie winces, and I immediately feel like an asshole. I truly am not hard-bitten or soulless enough to see anything even remotely humorous in the deaths of four innocents. Hell, nobody deserves to die like that, not even the guilty. It's just the business I'm in. This is my second stint on night cops, and if what I cover is any indication, the human race is getting nastier by the year. Sometimes sick humor is all the salve you've got.

"Sorry," I say. Wheelie looks surprised. He is not used to hearing me apologize, even if I should once in a while.

"I've got a meeting with the suits," he says. "I'll check with you when I get back, in two hours if I'm lucky."

I remind him that he is a suit now. He gives me a dirty look, then glances at his watch, says "shit," and scurries for the elevator.

Wheelie's a busy man these days. He's filling two seats, at least until corporate finds a replacement for Grubby.

Oh, yeah. I forgot to mention: Grubby's dead.

The publisher and I had our problems, but, like those four girls, Grubby didn't deserve the demise he met.

Death by Segway. Good lord.

Why do we even have Segways? They seem worthless as a broke-dick dog to me, equally useless on streets and sidewalks, to say nothing of being just a tad dangerous. I vaguely remember them being foisted upon us as the biggest thing since dental floss, but I have not seen the light. When the company CEO drove one off a cliff and got his ass killed three years ago, that kind of sealed the deal for me. When I see a cop or some other public servant riding one of them because he has to, I can read the little thought balloon over his head: "I look like an asshole." Maybe it's a West Coast thing. I don't know. I just know we're shy a publisher right now because of them.

Chip Grooms saw the whole thing. James H. Grubbs himself was the one who told Wheelie to be sure we had a photographer on the scene, and Grooms drew the short straw.

It was supposed to be a "bonding" experience. Grubby organized it. The idea was to get city and county officials together (along with area big shots, a group into which Grubby self-qualified himself) to do something "fun." The hope was that the city and county people, whose cooperation skills are on the Sunni-Shiite level, would have a Kumbaya moment and realize we all really can get along. As if. In a state where cities aren't part of counties and can't annex any of that Yuppie-rich suburban land, localities don't have to get along. And so they don't, enthusiastically.

In the end, the only bonding that got done was Grubby bonding with the GRTC Number Eleven bus on its way from the Capitol to Mosby Court.

They did it down in Shockoe Bottom. Grooms said he overheard the instructions the Segway master gave beforehand to the assembled officials. They could have stressed the danger a little more clearly, he told us, but where's the fun in that?

The big thing the Segway guy emphasized (and maybe Grubby didn't hear it because he was busy trying to be our region's catalyst, maybe breaking up a fistfight between a county commissioner and a city councilwoman) was the part about getting on and off the contraptions.

You have to do your dismount by grabbing the vertical bar with both hands. If you only hold it with one hand and hold on to the handlebar with the other, as conditioning and common sense might indicate you should, and then you put one foot on the ground, the thing behaves more or less like a bucking bronco, dragging you around in circles until you fall free or just fall.

Grubby, who employed the proscribed one-foot-at-a-time method, just fell. It was, Grooms said, kind of like those deals where the captain gets thrown overboard and the unmanned boat does endless 360s, coming back to the same spot to terrorize the poor sap floundering in the water.

Grubby was run over by his own Segway. That wasn't the bad part, though. In an effort to get out of the way of the relentless whirling dervish, he rolled out into Main Street just as Number Eleven was making its half-hourly appearance.

If the bus had only been on time, Grubby would still be with us, Mark Baer observed.

"What," Enos Jackson wondered, "are the odds of a city bus being on time?"

It wasn't pretty. I am fairly sure that Grubby's untimely demise won't make the city and county folks work together any better than they did before, even though everyone said all the right things afterward.

Grubby was not a bad man. He never fired me, despite the many opportunities I gave him. My main sorrow is that he devoted all that brainpower to the gods of corporate skull-duggery instead of remaining an honest newspaperman, which is what he used to be.

It turned out Grubby had very little family, just a mother out in the Midwest somewhere. As is our wont in Virginia, we probably will erect a historical marker somewhere, perhaps not mentioning the Segway incident.

And so Wheelie, who admits he is "not cut out for this kind of shit," is now thrust into the role. Well, not thrust. He could have said no, but Wheelie, though he's still a newspaperman, worries me sometimes. He could be turned, I think, if the paycheck was big enough. Most of us could.

Somebody suggested that we form a "team" to go full-bore into the Tweety Bird killings. Upon further review, though, we realized that we don't really have enough "players" any more to form a team. With all the layoffs, cut hours, furloughs and such, we're about a shortstop and a center fielder shy.

I have been told, though, that Mark Baer and Sarah Goodnight will be contributing to the effort, when they can find time away from their regular beats, which take up all the forty hours they get paid for and then some.

Baer and Sarah come by to see what they can do. There's plenty, but I've got to bring them up to speed. It seems to be up to me, being older than both of them combined, to be the leader of our team lite, and I am not exactly the greatest choice for that role. I've known lots of reporters over the years who decided at some point that they'd rather be assholes than work for one. Some of them have become my bosses. All I want to do, all I've ever wanted to do, is wrestle the news to the ground, tie it in a nice bundle, and get it printed on A1 with my name on it.

Frankly some make the switch because they wake up one day and realize they aren't cut out for chasing that breaking-news ball five million times, all the way to retirement. They run out of adrenaline, or they just want a life.

Sarah still thinks she is cut out for it. I probably should try to steer her in other directions. I have seen what happens when you list "reporter" as your occupation for more than three decades and really give a shit. I see the evidence every morning when I shave.

Baer, he's a different case. He still has dreams of working at the *Washington Post* or the *New York Times* someday, but reality might be setting in. I've seen him in Wheelie's office a couple of times lately with the door shut. There's always an editing job available, even in these lean and hungry times. He might be settling, as in settling for being an editor here as opposed to being a reporter here, just in case that *Post* thing doesn't work out.

"I thought I could maybe try to track down some of the girls' parents," Baer says. "See how they've been dealing with all this."

I tell him that sounds like a good idea. It'll keep him out of my hair at least. I think, as the father of a twenty-three-year-old daughter, that I know how they're dealing with it. But I'll let Baer find that out for himself. He goes off to start making calls.

Sarah wants to talk to some of the girls and young women who might be in harm's way. Sounds fine to me.

"Just be careful," I tell her.

"I'm always careful," she says. "And I bet you wouldn't even be telling me that if I weren't a woman."

"When this SOB starts murdering young guys, I'll even tell Baer to be careful."

"Sorry. But I am really pissed about this. I hope they catch him and cut his balls off."

She notices the look I give her.

"What?"

"Is that the same mouth you used to kiss your mommy and daddy good night with?"

"You are an idiot," she says as she turns to leave, "and a hypocrite."

Could be. She's got just as much right to be a potty-mouth as I do.

The police aren't talking about that mysterious visitor at Havana 59, the one who enlisted my daughter's aid to lure the night watchman from the train station. They're going to want to talk to *everyone* who's ever drunk a mojito there, hoping to get some kind of lead on this thing. They need some kind of bone to throw the public, some indication that they are on the case. They think it will be much better, I believe, channeling the mind of Chief L.D. Jones, if they come up with some kind of bullshit artist's sketch of the guy rather than just saying a mysterious stranger might be involved in the Tweety Bird murders.

Unfortunately for them, they won't have that luxury.

The chief and his minions will read, in tomorrow's paper, what they already know but haven't seen fit to share with the public: Some guy at a bar made sure the night watchman at the train station left his post for thirty minutes or maybe an hour, and in that time, a dead girl's body was delivered to the station.

I hope the cops don't try to take it out on Andi. I don't think there is a law against not telling the police your father is a journalist.

It might be worth calling the chief or one of his flacks to ask them to confirm what I already know about the stranger at Havana 59. The chief won't confirm anything, though, just sputter something about an ongoing investigation. Much better to let him read about it in tomorrow morning's paper and spit his cornflakes wondering if he has a snitch in his department. I have to make sure not to call Peachy Love on anything resembling a traceable line any time soon.

THERE ISN'T MUCH going on, considering it's a warm Friday night. The city has undergone a renaissance in recent years, meaning that it has stopped losing population and shows signs of not becoming Detroit South. The downside of that is that a bunch of mostly white yuppies renting in what used to be abandoned tobacco warehouses down in the Bottom are now interacting with Richmond's entrenched and often impoverished African American community. Sometimes when this happens, there are cultural misunderstandings. Some of the newly minted college grads with suburban upbringings don't understand that, when a skinny fourteen-year-old kid points a gun at you and demands your wallet, it really doesn't work to channel your inner John Wayne.

"Motherfucker tried to grab my gun," I heard one kid say in court, on trial for malicious wounding. "I didn't have no choice."

Tonight, though, is quiet. After I write my story on Jessica Caldwell and the latest Tweety Bird murder, I slip out and take a quick drive down to the Bottom.

It's only ten, too early for the party-hearty set and just about the time geezers my age are leaving the restaurants.

I find a parking space two blocks away from Havana 59, planning to drop in on Andi. On the north side of Franklin Street, the land is still waiting to be developed. I'm not sure it needs to be developed. There's all kinds of hell being raised about a project to bring a Target or Walmart or some such shit in there. In addition to the fact that it would create a Grade Five clusterfuck along the exit and entrance to I-95, there's our city's constant companion: history. Seems that, underneath the dirt and concrete, between here and the railroad tracks, an unknown number of former slaves are buried, no doubt in unmarked graves. This was pretty much Ground Zero for the early slave trade that stains our city like some indelible birthmark that all the face powder in the world can never hide.

A former state senator, guy named Wat Chenault, is fronting for a bunch of bright-eyed hustlers who claim they'll grow the tax base and make "shabby" Shockoe Bottom shine like a diamond. Chenault actually used that word, "shabby." It didn't sit well with people, myself included, who think the Bottom's adequate for our entertainment purposes. For those a couple or three decades younger than me, it's a pretty cool place, if you don't look at it too hard in the daylight. And most of us are pretty sure Chenault and his gang are only interested in growing their own personal economies.

Chenault and I have some history, going back to my first stint as night cops reporter, back in the early eighties. When the recent plan to bring big boxes to the Bottom first hit, complete with a breathless story by one of our business writers and artist's renderings that included everything except goddamned unicorns and baby pandas, I revisted some of Wat Chenault's somewhat soiled history. I know most of it by heart, because I was there.

The story ("Developer once center/of legislative scandal") has led to threats of litigation, against me and the paper. This bothers the suits a lot. Lawyers are expensive.

Andi is mixing something I would never drink and costs about what six Millers run me at happy hour.

She doesn't see me at first, and I use the time to be parent voyeur, watching my first-and-only born keep up two different conversations while she mixes one drink and takes another order. I have spent much time in close proximity to bartenders over the years, and I'm not just being a proud dad when I say they don't get paid nearly enough.

"What are you doing here?" she says, overjoyed no doubt to see her dear old dad. I might have noted that, with her occupation and my habits, it had to happen.

I order a beer and explain that I was worried about whether the cops had been bothering her.

"Yeah," she says, "they came around to my place this morning, and one came by tonight. They're bothering the hell out of the customers. I can't tell them what I don't know, though. I never saw the dude, or if I did, I don't remember. There were about a million people in here Wednesday night."

"Do they know you're my daughter?"

"Oh, yeah. The one tonight, he actually asked me if I was Willie Black's daughter. I admitted that I was."

"Fat guy with red hair and a bad comb-over?"

"Yeah."

Gillespie might have noticed the physical resemblance between my daughter and me. I don't blame Andi for telling the truth, but I'm sure I'll be getting a call from one of Gillespie's superiors, maybe the chief himself, soon.

I check my phone when I leave half an hour later. Sure enough, there's a text message from Chief Jones. "Call me, now." The chief is apparently economizing. Nowhere close to 140 characters.

I turn my phone off and head back to the office. I'll let L.D. Jones read the morning paper before I call him back, by which time he probably won't want to speak to me anyhow.

CHAPTER THREE

Saturday

I have a lunch date with Cindy Peroni, which is, I hope, a step in the right direction.

We haven't seen much of each other since the unfortunate events of last year, when I managed to drink myself out of one of the best things to happen in my hapless life in some time. Cindy, little sister of my old Hill buddy Andy Peroni, decided she had enjoyed about as much of me as she could stand after a particularly unpleasant episode in which I punched a guy whose hand, I thought, was roaming a bit too far south on her lovely body. I made a bad situation infinitely worse by then calling her a very bad name. She knows I didn't mean it, but, like she said, life's too short. She's already been divorced from one loser. After a while, it starts to look like a trend.

But I'm trying to make a comeback. I'm easing up on the booze. I'm not smoking as much. I've sent flowers. I have wooed Cindy Peroni with more fervor than I may have exhibited toward any of my three ex-wives. I've even employed the services of my friend and her brother, for how much good that will do.

Maybe I'm just trying to make up for past transgressions. Maybe I'm getting too old and creaky to be the flaming asshole I once was.

Finally she agreed to meet me at The Strawberry Street Café, a nice, neutral place at a nice, neutral time, one P.M.

STRAWBERRY STREET IS packed when we arrive, separately. (Her choice, obviously.) It must be free lunch day, the way they're lined up outside. We wait twenty minutes, surrounded by strangers, and get a table flanked on one side by a group of six who seem to all be hard of hearing and on the other by a family with three small children.

Questions are repeated. Answers are repeated. Finally we finish our meal, get a check, and leave without settling anything.

I reach by habit for my habit, the Camels in my coat pocket. Cindy squelches a smile when she sees me stop and pretend I've totally given up tobacco.

"Go ahead," she says. "One more won't kill you. I mean, they all will, in their totality, but this one won't take more than another ten seconds off your life."

I'm scrambling for something to say that might bring global warming to the Ice Age I've made of our relationship. We can finally talk here, as I walk her back to her car.

"If every Camel I smoked took ten seconds off my life and, at the same time, gave me ten more seconds with you, I'd be up to four packs a day."

Obviously touched, she says, "You always could bullshit, Willie."

But it does cause at least a temporary thaw. I am able to give her further assurances that I am getting better with age, turning into fine wine instead of vinegar.

"I hardly ever drink anymore, and I've cut way back on the Camels."

Of course, this means two drinks a day instead of six and maybe six cigarettes instead of a pack.

She gives me an uncensored smile.

"Yeah, Andy said you weren't much fun anymore."

"Try me."

She looks at me and then looks away.

"Maybe. Let me think on it."

I resist the urge to tell her we're not getting any younger. Maybe I am growing brain cells in my old age.

We shoot the breeze awhile, her leaning on her car and me facing her. When she looks at her watch and says she has to be somewhere, I lean forward to kiss her. She lets me.

I DON'T HAVE to be at the paper for another hour, so I make a run by Peggy's. It's a nice day. It feels like fall even though the equinox is still a week away. Driving through Oregon Hill, I can hear televisions blaring through open windows, most tuned in to the Virginia Tech football game. At my mother's house, she, Andi and Awesome are all sitting on the porch, watching the world go by from their blue-collar perch.

They bring out another chair for me. Peggy is surreptitiously sharing a joint with Awesome, setting it on the edge of an ashtray with one hand and waving with the other as a cop car rolls by. She won't let Andi smoke anything now, thank God, until the baby comes. I politely decline, noting that I have to go to work and find it hard to make my fingers hit the right keys when I'm stoned.

"Suit yourself," my mother says, shrugging. "More for me."

I'm glad Andi's living here. I think it helps her as much as it does Peggy. With her cold-footed ex-boyfriend more or less out of the picture, and with her determined she's going to have this kid, come hell or high water, what better mentor could she have than Peggy Black, who raised her bouncing, mixed-race boy in bone-white Oregon Hill without anything like the family support group Andi has? Andi's mother, Jeanette Stone (once Black) Walker, sees her a couple of times a week and is probably more excited than Peggy at the prospect of being a grandmother. And Thomas Jefferson

Blandford V will, if nothing else, be good for the kind of child support my mother never saw.

As for Peggy, she's still reeling (as am I) over the loss of Les Hacker. She needs somebody to love and nurture. She's done it for me, for any number of worthless husbands and "uncles" who used to plague us and then leave or get thrown out, and she certainly did it for Les. Now, in her hour of need, she has Andi.

We get about forty minutes of quality time before I have to go punch the clock. Literally. The suits have put in this system by which we have to punch in and out, like we're working at the sawmill. It did no good, Sally Velez told me, to explain to them that reporters have weird hours, often off company property. It did no good to tell them that any good reporter will work far beyond the forty (or, in our case, thirty-seven and a half) hours for which we're paid.

So, it's up to people like Sally to spend time they might have spent doing actual journalism "fixing" the hours to make it look as if we're really in the office when we're out covering actual news. And the unintended (but fully expected, for anyone with shit for brains) consequence is that more and more editors, reporters, and photographers are working to the clock instead of working until it's done. A couple of times, copy editors have walked out on a Friday or Saturday night before everything was edited, because their workweeks were officially over. People will live down to your expectations, I want to tell whatever genius came up with this system.

As I walk off the porch, Awesome falls into step with me. This is unusual. The Dude is as friendly and generous as he is feckless, but he usually isn't what you'd call gregarious.

I wait for it. Finally he speaks.

"You know that fella, that Tweety Bird guy?"

I let him finish.

"I might of seen him."

This has my attention. Awesome sees a lot and remembers an amazing amount for a lifetime stoner.

"When?"

Awesome is often flummoxed by "when." Not this time.

"It was last year, about when they found that girl, found her body, over by Texas Beach."

I know that Awesome, who was at least partially homeless until Peggy and Les took him in, likes to stay in touch with his old, less fortunate acquaintances, sometimes taking them food and clothing, usually compliments of Peggy. In good weather, Texas Beach is one of his stops.

"It was, like, warm that day, so I went over there with some clothes and shit. And this fella, Red, had some pretty good weed, and we got to drinking and, first thing you know, it's dark, and I just stayed."

They were camped in the bushes down by the river, and it had turned cold as a gravedigger's ass, Awesome says.

"There wadn't nobody much else there," he says. He was lying in the dark, thinking about the warmth of Peggy's English basement, when he heard a scream.

"I was scared, Willie. There's some bad dudes down there sometimes."

He says he crawled up the hill a little and stumbled onto a path, another way to the river farther downstream.

"I can see good at night," Awesome says, "but it was dark as hell. I heard another couple of sounds, like maybe an animal or something, and then some little 'whirr-whirr' kind of sounds. And then I heard the bushes rustling, and I laid real still.

"Dude, he walked right by me. He couldn't of been ten feet away. I just about shit myself. And then he was gone."

I ask him what he did then.

"Soon as I felt safe, I got the fuck out of there."

He knows the night it happened for a good reason. Two days later, the searchers found Kelli Jonas's abused body around the place where that path would have met the James River.

"I never went back there," he says. "I run into Red a few months later, and he said the cops was all over him for a while, along with everybody else down there. He said he didn't tell 'em about me, which I appreciated.

"I know I shoulda gone to the cops, or told somebody, but I was scared. I didn't want nothing to do with any of that mess. The cops got it in for me anyhow."

The police did have a tendency, in Awesome's more feral days, of homing in on him. He's spent a few weeks in jail over the course of his troubled, drug-addled life.

"I thought they'd catch the son of a bitch," he says. We're standing by my car now, me smoking a Camel and the Dude talking.

"But they never did, and he keeps doin' it. I want it to stop, Willie, but they'll think I did it if I tell them now."

I ask Awesome if he remembers anything about the man.

"It was dark as shit. Couldn't hardly see my hand in front of my face. All I remember is seeing his feet when he walked by, not hurrying, like he was out on a damn picnic."

I don't know where, if anywhere, this is all leading. They already found footprints.

I tell the Dude to let me know if he remembers anything else.

"You ain't gonna tell the cops I was there, are you, Willie?"

The look of desperation fades when I tell him I won't.

"I just want to help," he says.

TALKING ABOUT THE Kelli Jonas case makes me wonder if Mark Baer's gotten around to calling her parents yet.

At the office, I see that Baer's spending his Saturday at his desk. For all his butt-kissing and ladder-climbing efforts, I have to admit that Baer does work. I am sure that the meter has already run out on his time-clock week.

"I called twice, but nobody answered, just got voice mail," he says. "They haven't called back yet."

There's nothing much going on in the newsroom. Most of Baer's compatriots ran out of hours sometime yesterday afternoon.

There are no dirt naps in my in-box yet, so I make an offer.

"How about if I drive by there?"

Baer surprises me by accepting my offer.

"I'm up to my ass, got two more stories to write. I'd appreciate it."

I tell Sally I'll be back in a while and to call my cell if mayhem erupts before sundown.

"Be sure and clock out," she says. Her hours are long since up, too, I'm thinking.

Between there and the front door, I forget, as usual.

The Jonases haven't moved since their daughter's murder. They live where they always have, in a western Henrico suburb that still has some life left before the renters start moving in, but it has seen better days. The new mall at Short Pump drew the developers and suburbanites west with it. The burbs keep moving west, and if you don't change houses every few years, you wake up one day and find that the nice little strip mall half a mile away now houses a nail salon, a judo studio, a payday loan operation and a bunch of For Lease signs.

Nobody answers when I knock, but I hear a lawn mower. I walk around to the side yard and there's a man, about my age, working his way around the Bradford pears with a push mower.

He cuts the mower when I make my presence known. When I tell him I'm from the newspaper, he doesn't immediately order me off the property.

"You want to talk about Kelli." It's not a question, but I answer anyhow.

"It's been eighteen months," I say, stating the obvious, "and we thought we ought to check back, see how you're handling it and all."

He takes off his ball cap and wipes the sweat from his brow. He's going bald on top, and when he takes off his sunglasses, his eyes are those of a man who isn't sleeping anything like the full eight hours. He looks like somebody who went from fifty years old to sixty in about a week.

"'Handling it,'" he says, and lets out something that sounds like a laugh, only without the humor. "Man, you don't handle this. My wife will never get over this. I will never get over this. I come inside sometimes and Cathy will be sitting in Kelli's room, going through her stuff, like she can figure this all out somehow, like she can find something there that will make it stop hurting.

"She was our only child. We are childless now. And they can't even catch the bastard."

Mr. Jonas says the police do check by once in a while, but nothing they tell him makes him think they're anywhere close to catching his daughter's killer.

"They might as well have just broken into our house and killed us all," he says. "And your paper just moves on to somebody else's nightmare."

There really isn't anything else he can tell me that the cops and our readers don't already know. When I ask if I can take a picture of him or him and his wife with my nifty new iPhone camera, he finally tells me to get off the property.

Back in the car, I think about Andi. I almost told the grieving father I had a daughter about Kelli's age but then realized how truly hurtful and stupid that would be.

It would be beyond trite to tell Mr. Jonas I can feel his pain. But in a small way, I can. I want Mr. Tweety Bird drawn and fucking quartered, with all the parents of the dead girls present. Still if I put my pinkie toe into one of the Jonases's shoes, I know it wouldn't do a damn bit of good.

I'd like to do it, though. Some people just need to die.

CHAPTER FOUR

My phone rings as I'm pulling back on the street. I have been conned into buying an iPhone, and it's about three times as worthless as my old fliptop, which spent its last year held together by duct tape. The iPhone's great for getting e-mail and texting and taking pictures and looking up the halftime score to the Virginia-Carolina game. As a phone, it's worthless as tits on a bull. I have to swerve to the curb in order to achieve the manual dexterity to answer the damn thing.

"Where are you?"

Wheelie sounds somewhat frantic. I tell him what I'm doing.

"Well, you need to get your ass back here. Wat Chenault's in my office."

Shit.

"Do we want to talk to him?"

"We want to not get sued, I'm pretty sure about that."

I tell Wheelie I'll be there in ten minutes. It's probably fifteen, but Wheelie can wait, and fuck Wat Chenault.

"Don't do anything to make this worse," our editor warns me.

I tell him I won't, but my fingers are crossed.

Poor Wheelie. He came down here from Providence full of hope and promise, aiming to win us a Pulitzer. With his staff shrunk considerably by the Great Recession and some incredibly bad business decisions by the Suits Who Never Suffer, he's had a hard time just keeping our nose above water. The bleeding has gone from ruptured aorta status to a slow drip, but it can't be any fun being Wheelie these days. And now, with Grubby gone and no plans to hire a new publisher, he's farther into the heart of corporate darkness than he ever thought he'd have to venture. But, hey, he didn't turn down the extra money.

When I get to the newsroom, one Camel later, I go up to the fourth floor, where Wheelie hangs his coat these days, only wandering down to the newsroom on most days for the ten A.M. and three P.M. meetings.

I see the back of Wat Chenault's head and, across the desk, Wheelie's earnest face nodding in agreement to something—probably something he shouldn't be agreeing to.

Wheelie motions for me to come in.

"I guess you know Willie Black," he says.

Wat Chenault gives me the once-over and says, "I expect I do."

Chenault was a football player in college. He was a wide receiver, but nowadays the main thing that's wide is his ass. He looks like one of those lard-butt middle guards you see in the NFL games, the ones who stop the running attack by just throwing their fat guts into the middle of the action like sumo wrestlers and letting the runners bounce off them. Christ, he must weigh 350 pounds. His face is as wide as it is high, with little piggy eyes peeking out from under bushy gray eyebrows. He's wearing a UVA polo shirt with orange horizontal stripes, as if he searched long and hard in his closet for the one thing that could make him look more obese than he already is.

He is a homegrown product, as Virginia as blue crabs and massive resistance. He grew up in one of those sleepy towns down in peanut country, about as Heart of Dixie as anywhere in the commonwealth. After college he was a natural choice to be a state politician, with his jock creds, family money and old-boy ties. He got elected the first time despite having falsely claimed that he played for the Washington Redskins. In reality, the team used Wat for a tackling dummy for a couple of weeks in August before sending him back to the Southside. He could slap you on the back and make you feel like he gave a shit. And the ex-jock thing, even if he did gild the lily, didn't hurt.

He was the kind of guy who you always knew could be counted on to tell a racist joke, if he knew only "his" people were listening. I have to admit that he did not endear himself to me in my days covering the legislature when I heard, third-hand, that he had taken to referring to me, after a few bourbon-and-waters, as "Woodshed Willie," his humorous reference to my mixed-race heritage.

He advanced from the House of Delegates to the State Senate, and he was considering a run at attorney general, gateway to the governor's mansion, back in 2001 when his political career went farther south than an Antarctic expedition.

The girl he was caught with was fourteen years old. I still remembered her name when I reintroduced our readers to the story: Leigh Adkins. He swore she said she was eighteen, and maybe she did. But when you're a forty-six-year-old state senator and you slip a girl who "says" she's eighteen into your room at a boutique hotel favored by the pols, you might expect somebody to talk. One of our young lions got a tip from a friend who ran the night desk there. He borrowed a camera from photo, took a seat near the elevator, unscrewed the nearest lightbulb, and waited five hours in the twilight before Ms. Adkins, accompanied by the senator and looking somewhat used, came around the corner.

He managed to take the picture and run down the stairs before Wat Chenault could catch him. Even then, Wat wasn't doing a real fast forty-yard dash. The picture pretty much told the story, but we managed to track down Leigh Adkins. Actually I was the one who got a call from her sister, who was somewhat pissed. Leigh was, it turned out, one of Chenault's constituents and a former babysitter of his. The sister had an apartment in Bon Air. She worked down at the Capitol and took little Leigh in one day to see the sausage being made. They visited the office of her old employer, the senator, and the girl must have been overcome by the aphrodisiac of power. The sister somehow let him take her to a party, which turned into a rather intimate gathering at the boutique hotel, where Wat presumably showed her the sausage.

The young buck and I had a dual byline. He's at the *Los Angeles Times* now, so I was left to be Mr. Institutional Memory and remind our readers of just what a scumbag Wat Chenault was if not is.

It kind of drove a stake through Chenault's political career. He was lucky to avoid jail. A good lawyer can get you out of just about anything. He pleaded contributing to the delinquency of a minor or some such bullshit, but other stories of Wat's misdeeds between the sheets with the younger set started drifting into the public domain, and he chose not to run for reelection. He retreated to his family's lumber business, got into home building and then development. Everything that goes around comes around, and here's Wat Chenault, twelve years later, trying to turn the blighted Bottom into an urban paradise and, coincidentally, make a nice little bundle for himself on the side.

"Like I was saying," Chenault says, turning his massive self back toward Wheelie and forgoing the opportunity to reminisce about the good old days with me, "I'm not looking for revenge here, but when you write things about me that damage me financially . . ."

"How about if they're true?"

Wheelie frowns. I should just keep my damn mouth shut, but diplomacy has never been my strong suit.

Chenault's neck turns a spectacular color of purple, somewhere around eggplant. He swivels sharply in my direction and looks like he wants to jump out of that seat and throw a block, driving me through the plate-glass window and into the hallway. I take half a step back, but it's probably too much trouble for him to get his ass up.

He lets go of the chair arms and turns back to Wheelie.

"You all have been malicious. There wasn't any reason to bring up my youthful indiscretions."

I bite my tongue hard on "youthful indiscretions." The only thing "youthful" about Wat Chenault's indiscretion was the barely teenage girl he was sweating on in that hotel room.

"What's that got to do with the Top of the Bottom project?" he says.

That's what they're calling it: Top of the Bottom. "Mixed-use" is the magic term they're using these days. Somehow they hope to get the Targets and Best Buys, maybe even, praise God, a Walmart, to come to a part of the city that wasn't even full-time habitable until they built the floodwall to keep out the James River back in 1995.

They'll fill the rest of the space with overpriced rental properties for the ones too young or too old to have school-aged children at home. The city is a lot of things, many of them good. It is not anybody's idea of an educational mecca. The kids turn six and you can't go the freight for private school, it's time for what Chuck Apple, my stand-in on night cops, calls a Helen Keller Colonial in Chesterfield County.

"Hell," Chuck said when I asked for enlightenment, "old Helen could find her way around any one of them once she'd been in one. Every one of 'em's exactly alike."

Wheelie tries to explain that what he did in disinterring the past is fair game.

"We never accused you of doing something you didn't do."

"Ah," he says, and I know that, in Chenault's mind at least, he's got us. "You wrote that I was a felon. What I pleaded to wasn't no damn felony. It was a misdemeanor. You called me a felon!"

My heart does a little tom-tom number. I don't remember calling him a felon, even if he is one. He just hired a good enough lawyer to get what started out as a felony watered down.

Then he hauls a copy of our A section out of his briefcase.

"How about this?" he says, and I breathe easier, although this won't make Wheelie's load any lighter. He's circled a sentence on our editorial page from two weeks ago. I never read the damn editorials. Looking over Chenault's massive shoulder, I can see that our first-floor thinking class wrote: "Mr. Chenault has come far since his unfortunate and felonious fall from grace, but we question the wisdom of his project." (They call 'em "Mr." and "Mrs." and sometimes even "Ms." in editorials, no matter how big an SOB they are. They might wish you to burn in hell, but they'll never disrespect your title.)

Jesus. For once editorial and I are on the same page, and somehow they managed to fuck it up. If only we had copy editors. Those mossbacks of my youth, whom I despised for their persnickety arrogance but also because they were almost always right, never would have let that one get through. Somebody in editorial didn't do due diligence.

Wheelie does the hummina-hummina and then says we'll certainly run a retraction. I'm pretty sure that isn't going to be enough for Wat Chenault, who must have a pretty good hard-on for us for helping him ruin his political career all those years ago.

When our large guest isn't appeased, Wheelie counters by offering a correction on A1. Fuck it, I want to tell my editor and erstwhile publisher. You and I both knew what Chenault wants. And it's a damn sight more than a little groveling on the front page.

The fat man does not disappoint.

"What I want," he says, drumming his thick right forefinger on the desk for emphasis and lowering his voice like he thinks the walls might be bugged, "is for you all to leave me the fuck alone."

He means, of course, turn a blind eye to Top of the Bottom, even come out foursquare in favor of the thing we were against the day before.

To Wheelie's credit, he doesn't cave instantly. He says we could certainly do a feature on Chenault. It's understood that this would be a puff piece, one of those "Catching up with . . ." pieces our features department does from time to time on somebody who used to be somebody. I'm thinking that, if I were Wat Chenault, I might not exactly want people catching up with me.

Chenault shakes his head.

"Not good enough, Wheelie."

"Even if we did, uh, back off our opposition to your project, Mr. Chenault, we can't tell the editorial department what to do."

Shit, Wheelie, I'm thinking, don't call him Mr. Chenault when he's calling you by your nickname. Don't cede ground you don't have to. Makes you look like a little boy called to the principal's office.

Chenault isn't buying what Wheelie's selling.

"Hell, man," he says, raising his voice enough that Sandy McCool, the administrative assistant, can probably hear him through the walls, "you're the goddamned publisher. Show some balls."

My estimation of Chenault's IQ just dropped below freezing. Like a lot of guys who aren't totally, completely sure of their power, Wheelie does not relish having his manhood challenged in front of others. In the past, I have made the same mistake Wat Chenault's just made.

Wheelie stands up. He isn't up to eggplant, but he's a nice shade of pink.

Chenault begins to haul his considerable avoirdupois out of his chair, not sure what's going on.

"I think our conversation is over, Mr. Chenault," Wheelie says. "We have our newspaper to run, and you have your priorities. We will run a correction on A1. We will, if you desire, do a nice story on your, er, comeback. Beyond that, I can promise you nothing."

"You will be hearing from my lawyer," Chenault says. I step out into the hallway so he can get past. He barely squeezes through the door.

"I expect we will," Wheelie says with a sigh. He doesn't bother to say good-bye or walk Chenault to the elevator. When our ex-senator walks past me, he stops for a second while he fishes a cigar out of his coat pocket, one he's probably going to light up on the elevator of our no-smoking building.

"You and I," he says, lowering his voice again and wagging the stogie at me, "we aren't through yet."

I walk back into the office to congratulate Wheelie for doing the exact thing Wat Chenault wanted him to do: show some cojones. My boss doesn't look nearly as satisfied as I would have been in his shoes.

"Damn, Willie," he says, "the suits are going to have my butt when this gets out. Maybe we ought to back off a little."

"Stay the course, Chief," I tell him. "You can't let that fat fuck push you around." I can tell that he likes it that I call him "Chief." Sounds a little more John Wayne than "Wheelie."

"Easy for you to say," he mutters. He's right. I've been nearly fired so many times, in addition to being demoted back to night cops, that they pretty much expect me to screw up. They expect better things from Wheelie. The difference between him and me? Wheelie still thinks he has a capital-C career. I'm just trying to keep drawing a paycheck for doing what I like: Sticking my big honker into other people's business until the bullshit is dispersed.

I leave.

I know Wheelie is troubled. If he's on the same side as me, he knows something must be terribly wrong.

I CHECK WITH Peachy Love, calling her on her private cell rather than her phone at headquarters, and find out that either the police have no new information on the latest Tweety Bird murder or—more likely—they don't choose to share their information with me.

I don't press Peachy on it. I don't want to impose on the good nature of my old friend, former colleague, and sometime playmate. Peachy was a good night cops reporter herself before she decided she'd rather work with the police than follow them around with a notepad and a digital camera. She often feeds me information that a good media-relations person really should keep to herself, but she and I know she has to pick her spots. If something's in the works, Peachy probably will find a way to let me know. Stonewalling me on the day-to-day stuff is how she keeps her credibility.

"Don't leave me in the dark, Peachy."

"Have I ever?"

AT ELEVEN THIRTY, when I'm about to call it a night and make an appearance at Penny Lane in time for a beer or three, we get word of a shooting, and I'm scrambling down to the Bottom. When I get there, I suss out the sad but too-familiar story. A party celebrating a birthday was stumbling out of one of our finer establishments just as another group, celebrating Saturday, emerged from the one next door. Somebody bumped somebody, maybe scuffed his shoe. Words were spoken. The testosterone kicked in. At least one of the participants had a gun. And someone's nineteen-year-old, underage drinking son is in the VCU Medical Center, clinging to a life that ought to have been good for another sixty years.

The gut-shot boy's friends are still there, leaning against cars, scared and pissed off.

"If I'd had a gun," one of them says, his eyes red, "I'd of shot the son of a bitch."

It is our answer to everything. The shooter, already caught and locked up, has a right to carry a people-popping firearm. All hail the Second Amendment. And since he has one, the kid who might have a confrontation with him outside some bar has to have one, too. A gun for a gun. Old Testament meets the Wild West.

When I was a kid, back in the day, we had fights in Oregon Hill all the time. I'd had my nose broken twice by the time I was fifteen. Almost all of the fights involved fists, so much so that the Hill has turned out more than its share of boxers over the decades. It was considered the street equivalent of going nuclear if one of you pulled a knife.

It takes more balls than most of our young studs possess to cut somebody to death. It gets a little messy. And it's damn near impossible to beat somebody to death with your fists.

Whoever is perpetuating our street-level arms race, I'm thinking there's a toasty little corner of hell that has their names all over it.

I'M ABLE TO get the folks at Havana 59 to let me sit at a table with my beer and e-mail my story back on my laptop. I mishit the tiny little keys about every fourth time. Still it's better than driving all the way back to the paper. I look up after I've sent my story, and there's Andi, behind the bar. I didn't think she was working tonight.

She's off at one, so we have time to talk for a couple of minutes before she drives back to Peggy's and I go back to my humble abode.

"The cops were by again," she says. "They showed me a couple of pictures, wanted to know if I'd seen either one of them. But I wasn't able to help them."

"Sounds like they might be on somebody's trail."

"I don't know. I'll leave that cops-and-robbers stuff to you."

I tell her to get off her feet. She needs her rest.

"Jeez, Dad. I'm pregnant. I'm not an invalid."

Ah, youth. Even as kids not much younger than she is are being murdered by lunatics and shooting holes in each other, Andi thinks nothing bad could possibly happen to her.

Why worry?

That's what fathers are for.

CHAPTER FIVE

Sunday

Abe and I are watching the Redskins lose when Peachy calls.

"Do you know a guy named Ronnie Sax?"

I do.

Ronnie Sax was before Peachy's short time as an honest journalist. He was a good photographer, but kind of squirrelly, or am I being redundant? He came to the paper as Ron Kusack. Two or three years later, he let it be known that he was Ronnie Sax. I guess he thought it would stand him better in his later career as a famous photojournalist, which never developed, pardon the pun. Or maybe he just thought—mistakenly—that it would make him a Cool Dude.

He's done a lot of freelancing of different sorts since he and the paper parted company. I run across a photo he's taken from time to time in Richmond's weekly entertainment magazine or one of the other rags trying to make a living off ink and paper. Last year he was shooting a wedding I got dragged to.

It's all starting to come back to me now.

Ronnie was not trustworthy. He was suspected a couple of times of staging "spontaneous" photos. Back then before the hanging judges of human resources started calling the shots, you could take somebody like Sax, a guy who had talent enough for you to overlook his less savory qualities, and give him a stern talking-to, off the books, and let it go at that. Turns out we should have just fired his ass.

Even in those lenient days, many of us were not sure that Ronnie hadn't already used up all the strikes a budding photojournalist should have.

Strike three, though, was a doozy.

It turns out that Ronnie Sax was doing a bit of freelancing while he was still drawing a paycheck from the paper. And some of his freelancing, a rather lucrative part of it, was porn.

The end came soon after a well-endowed West End couple discovered that their darling daughter, a sophomore at the University of Richmond who also was well-endowed, was featured rather prominently in a movie they had rented to add a little zest to their love life. Confronted, she finally and tearfully told all. Ronnie Sax, it turns out, had managed to talk her into doing a couple of "glamour" shoots—part of glamour, apparently, being buck naked in a gynecological pose. He had then introduced her to a friend who was in the porn business, and little Susan was soon stashing away some considerable bucks that she didn't even need in exchange for doing the nasty in front of a camera crew. It wasn't too hard to figure out that it was a local production. I saw one of their classics—purely for research, of course. The girl went by the stage name of Renee Wett, and the title was *Renee Ravages Richmond*. Kind of derivative, but the scene at the foot of the Lee Monument was pretty gripping.

As the father of a daughter, I think now that, in a similar situation, I might have shot Ronnie Sax. No one did, but we all knew the guy had to go. They raided his apartment and found lots of incriminating evidence. What they seized involved girls who were "legal," although in some cases barely so.

"Jesus," Peachy says, "I think I do remember somebody telling me about that guy. Well, it seems as if he still has a knack for snatch shots."

Somebody gave the cops a tip. It turns out that Ronnie Sax is living in an apartment in one of the converted warehouses down in the Bottom. He's been living there for about two years. And he bragged to a few of his neighbors that he had some "hot chicks" in for photo shoots. He even showed them some of the pictures. At least one of the neighbors was concerned enough about Ronnie's hobby, and that neighbor called the police. He said he thought one of the naked ladies bore a striking resemblance to Kelli Jonas, Tweety Bird Victim Number One.

"They brought him in for questioning this morning," Peachy tells me. "I don't think they can hold him, but they're pretty excited over this one."

No doubt they are. Chief L.D. Jones would love to close this particular file. The mayor gave a statement yesterday. It didn't exactly encourage the chief to start sending out résumés if a perp wasn't produced posthaste, but you could kind of see where the buck was going to stop—right in the chief's ample lap.

I thank Peachy and ask her to keep me posted. I promise to come around for a drink sometime soon. Encouraged to be more specific, I give a weasel answer.

"What the fuck," she says. "Are you swearing off chocolate?"

Straddling the racial lines that divide our lovely city even at this late date, I face different expectations from various constituencies. It seems clear to me that Peachy Love thinks I'm going Oreo on her, although it's more like bronze on the outside and white on the inside in my case.

At any rate, I assure my old friend and reliable source that this is not the case and that I am, as always, an equal opportunity fornicator.

"Couldn't prove it by me," she says. I detect a note of huffiness in her voice. I promise to come by sometime soon.

Truth is, I really do want it to work with Cindy Peroni, and I imagine that Cindy, while generous to a fault, probably isn't too cool on the subject of sharing. Of course I still haven't earned a second chance from the lovely Cindy. I'm working on that.

I figure the cops won't keep Ronnie Sax long unless he breaks down and admits he's a serial killer.

It doesn't take much—just a look at switchboard.com—to find Ronnie's address.

ABE HASN'T MOVED since I went into the den to take Peachy's call. He looks exasperated.

"Skins suck," is all the information I need.

SUNDAY AFTERNOON IN the Bottom is quiet. A few people are wandering out of their late brunches at Millie's or Poe's Pub. Farther down the river, they'll be sipping wine and contemplating the river at the newer places that have sprung up along with overpriced condos along the James.

I find Sax's apartment. No one answers when I knock, and I can't hear anything inside that might indicate anyone's there.

There's a pool outside, not far from the apartment. It's still warm enough to sit there and soak up some rays. I decide to wait. No one's checking IDs, although my age might hint to an observant person that I am a little outside the age range of most of the residents.

There are only two other people poolside. Then a young woman sits down two deck chairs from me. She takes off her robe. She's wearing a string bikini. I try not to stare.

After a few quiet moments, she turns to me.

"Do you live here?"

I tell her that I am an acquaintance of Ronnie Sax's and was supposed to meet him at his apartment.

"But it looks like he's been detained."

The girl gives me the stink-eye.

"Yeah," she says. "He's been detained, all right. The cops came by around eight. Woke my ass up. Do you know what that's all about?"

I confess that I am a reporter. I don't tell her that Ronnie Sax might be the reason half the women in Richmond are packing heat and the other half are carrying mace. No sense in getting everybody's knickers in a knot. I just tell her that I got a tip and am checking it out.

She's a smart girl, though.

"Ohmigod," she says, bringing her right hand up to her ample cleavage. "It's that Tweety Bird thing, isn't it? Damn. I knew there was something wrong with that dude."

She's heard the second-hand reports that he was doing some clothing-optional photo shoots in his apartment. I don't say it, but I'm surprised he hasn't approached Miss Buns here. Maybe she's too old for him, probably pushing thirty.

I emphasize that they are just questioning Sax.

"But, you're not, like, a friend or something?" she asks. She seems to be inching her chair a little farther from me.

I assure her I am not, although Ronnie Sax and I did work together, long ago, at the newspaper.

I ask her if she has any idea where he might have been last Wednesday night or Thursday morning. She says she doesn't.

A few minutes later, there's a commotion behind us. I turn to see three policemen escorting Ronnie Sax back to his apartment.

"You got no right to search," he says. One of the cops flashes a warrant in front of him.

"This says I do."

Obviously, they've questioned Ronnie already and have let him go, for now. But they're going on a little search party. I am sure Ronnie Sax's computer will be leaving the premises shortly.

"I already told you where I was," he says. "My sister will vouch for me."

"No doubt," one of the other cops says.

When I approach, one of them moves to intercept me. I tell them I'm a friend of Ronnie's, hoping the fetching lass behind me doesn't now think I'm not trustworthy.

"You're that asshole from the paper," the oldest of the three, and the guy in charge, says. I've seen him around, and I'm pretty sure he knows just what a pain in the butt I've been to Richmond's finest in the recent past.

Yeah, I confess, that's me.

Ronnie tells me to fuck off, but then he makes the connection.

"Willie Black!" he says, suddenly glad to see anyone who might not think he's a psychopath.

RONNIE SAX HAS an overbite and bad teeth. He's short, about five foot seven I'm guessing, and he's got this wheezy kind of laugh that generally adds to the creepiness. All I can think is he must be paying well to get women to let him take pictures of their lady parts.

I'm remembering something now. Once, a thousand years ago, the paper decided that everybody, even the statehouse reporters, of which I was one, had to produce x-number of feature stories. I think it was one a month.

Anyhow I saw that our last surviving local porn theater was having a real live porn star on the premises to autograph stuff and show her tits. I chose that for my puff piece of the month. They assigned Sax to go with me.

The woman looked like she was forty and was, according to her extensive résumé, twenty-six. She was pleasant enough, although most of what she said was later paraphrased.

"Jesus," Enos Jackson, my old editor, told me when he read the very rough draft. "You can't say 'pussy' in the paper."

But I remember Sax taking an inordinate amount of interest in her and asking her questions that were inappropriate even by my low standards.

Sax left before I did. When he was gone, the porn star said, "Who was that guy? He gives me the heebie-jeebies."

Hearing this, from a woman who made a living doing things in front of a camera that at least two of my three wives would never do in a dark room with their husband, made an impression.

"I don't know what these bastards are talking about," Ronnie says, as one of the bastards gives him what could only be described as a baleful look. "They've had it in for me ever since that thing back in 1992. That was twenty-one damn years ago."

I assure Ronnie that it'll all be straightened out soon.

"Well, it damn well better be," he says. "These assholes have ruined my reputation. I'm gonna sue."

He yells after the cop who's carrying out his computer.

"Hey, be careful with that. I got some valuable stuff in there."

"I bet," the cop says and warns Ronnie not to plan any big trips anytime soon.

According to Ronnie Sax, he had dinner with his sister and her kids on Wednesday night and didn't leave until after eleven. He also says he had a photo shoot on Thursday morning, across town.

"I've got witnesses," he says.

He asks me if I know a good lawyer. In exchange for a few more minutes gleaning some more background and quotes from Sax, I tell him he ought to contact Marcus Green. Marcus, with the aid of Kate Ellis, my third ex-wife, will be indebted to me, although he'd probably be looking up Ronnie Sax anyhow as soon as this breaks on the six o'clock news tonight. Marcus loves publicity more than a beagle loves bacon.

The background stuff is important: I want to be able to call the cops and tell them that I've had a long interview with Mr. Sax myself, and that he claims he had nothing to do with any of this and is going to sue them. Maybe then, after they get tired of threatening me for interfering with a police investigation, they'll tell me what they've got, or at least give me some bullshit quote, just so the story in tomorrow morning's paper doesn't look so one-sided.

I leave Ronnie Sax and head back to catch the second half of the four o'clock NFL game.

"Skins lost," Custalow informs me. Stop the presses.

I open a beer and get out the laptop. Until they start letting me drink openly in the office, I prefer to send stories I write on my off days from the comfort of my own rented abode.

I step into the other room and call Peachy, who tells me who the lead detective is on this case. Fella named Lombardo who I don't know that well. She gives me his number.

Lombardo knows who I am, which doesn't help us get off to a good start. Things go downhill when he learns that I've already interviewed Ronnie Sax.

"How the fuck did you know about that?" Obviously the cops who took Sax's computer didn't tell Lombardo I was there.

"Can I quote you? It'd make my boss happy to know I'm doing such a good job. He might even give me a raise."

Lombardo sputters a little. When he knows I'm serious about writing what Sax has told me, he finally calms down and gives me a passable quote about "ongoing investigation" and all that crap. He does confirm, though, that they're going over Sax's electronic records with the proverbial fine-tooth comb.

"You know, Black," he says before we part ways, "you're going to stick that big nose of yours where it doesn't belong one time too many and get it shot off one of these days."

I wish him a good evening.

I file the story, then put it onto our website. Someone else will put it into yet a third place, our tablet site, for which we are getting a few of our former readers to pay a very small amount. Print journalism, from where I sit, is trading dollars for dimes.

I go to bed early enough that Custalow asks me if I'm feeling well.

It's a fitful sleep. I keep thinking about Ronnie Sax, and about those girls. I haven't had a lot of interaction with psychopaths and sadists, but Mr. Sax had me fooled. I always thought of him, if I thought of him at all, as feckless and weak.

I didn't have Ronnie Sax pegged as pure evil, until now.

CHAPTER SIX

Monday

Peachy Love's call comes while I'm shaving.

"He's gone," she says.

Doesn't take a genius to figure out who "he" is.

The police, who had planned to call a press conference this morning announcing the arrest of a "person of interest" in the Tweety Bird murders, should have kept Ronnie Sax when they had the chance. When they popped around before six, planning to haul Sax away in his pajamas, he was, as Peachy Love said, long gone. Flown the coop. Tweety Bird takes wing.

It's eight thirty already, and I wonder what kind of damage control is going on. The chief must be needing adult diapers by now.

When I call headquarters, I'm told Chief Jones isn't in, won't be in and, it is understood, wouldn't piss on me if I were on fire even if he were, by some miracle, in. When I explain that I already know their prime suspect, left unattended overnight, is on the lam, and I further explain that all our readers who have iPhones or iPads also will know that shortly, there is quiet on the other end of the line.

I am promised a callback.

Not fifteen minutes later, I hear the blues-based ringtone on my phone. I am expecting some midlevel functionary giving me the latest self-serving comments from our highest-paid law-enforcement entity.

Instead it's L.D. Jones himself.

He probably was already pretty unhappy before he got the news that the entire metropolitan area, plus anyone who cared in the entire blogosphere, soon would know about his department's latest screwup. He's somewhere on the other side of sore pissed now.

"Black, goddamnit, you can't print that shit," he says by way of greeting. "It's unsubstantiated."

I tell him I'll take my chances.

"Where are you getting that crap from?"

I could just tell him it's none of his fucking business, but that might start him sniffing around possible leaks, including one staffer in particular who used to be a reporter.

So I make something up. I tell him that a woman I met yesterday at poolside, whose name I don't know, called me and told me she talked to someone who saw Sax leaving sometime in the middle of the night. I had left her my card and asked her to call me if she saw anything unusual concerning Mr. Sax. Miraculously she did.

"And," I go on, "knowing how proactive your department is, I just guessed you were going to arrest him today. Seems like I was right."

He doesn't know whether I'm being a wiseass about the "proactive" part.

"You don't know what we planned for today," he says. "You don't know your ass from first base."

"Well, I'll bet you a twenty that there was going to be a press conference called for this morning."

There is silence on the other end, followed by a sigh. I know that sigh. The chief is ready to switch gears and deal.

"Look, Willie," he says, changing over to first-name basis, going for a mix of friendliness and condescension, "this is off the record, but if you just wait a few hours, I'm sure we'll have this bastard all locked up. We know where he went. We're closing in on him even as we speak."

Like hell you are, I'm thinking but not saying. Finally, tiptoeing along that often-trod tightrope between what the police want and what our readers expect, I compromise. I'll post something about Sax apparently skipping town. No point in concealing his name, since it's in the story I wrote for this morning's paper. But I will write that there was nothing in Mr. Sax's background to indicate that he should have been locked up posthaste, so he was released. And, I'll add, when the cops got a look at his computer, they became much more interested in him and sent a SWAT team around to arrest him, by which time he had, of course, fled. I won't, in other words, write that our police are blithering idiots. The readers can infer.

"You did find something interesting in that computer, I'm assuming. Just keep quiet if I'm right."

Another sigh, but nothing else.

I tell the chief I'll even quote him as saying that the cops are sure they will have Sax in custody in a few hours.

L.D. Jones isn't happy with that, but he's happier than he would have been with my original plan, which was to spell out line by line just how easily our defenders let Sax slip away. He knows that I am cutting him a deal, and that I expect something in return.

"When you catch him," I say, letting the other shoe fall, "would you do me a favor and give me a heads-up?"

"Sure," he says. He sounds like he's saying it with his teeth clenched. I am sure that making a deal with the devil, meaning me, is taking a toll on the chief's molars.

I POST THE story online and then head down to the office, forfeiting yet another day off for the love of my sorry-ass job. Hell, I didn't have anything to do anyhow except maybe stop by and see Peggy.

I've already gotten a text message from Sally Velez. She's seen the story online and wants to know what I'm going to do for the "real paper."

The newsroom is pretty animated for eleven A.M. It almost seems like old times. One consequence of cutting people's hours from forty to thirty-seven and a half is that (a) people are working to the clock and (b) they tend to pile up hours early in the week and are mostly gone by Friday afternoon. So we're pretty bright-eyed and bushy-tailed on Monday mornings.

Sally calls me over and asks me what else I've got.

"Nothing I can write right now."

"Damn, Willie, that means you're holding out on me."

"Sorry. When we can print it, I'll write it."

She advises me that I'd better tell her what's going on, whether it gets in tomorrow morning's paper or not. She mentions that my testicles are in peril if I don't start talking.

So I tell her that the cops had him down there for at least four hours yesterday in interrogation, and that Sax said there wasn't any lawyer there. By the time the dumbass asked for one, they were ready to send him home anyhow. My guess is that they just screwed up, thought they could come back and arrest him later.

"And they found something on his computer?"

"My reliable source says so."

She leans close and whispers it.

"Peachy?"

Nobody's supposed to know that Peachy Love and I have contact beyond press conferences. As far as I can tell, Sally's the only one in the newsroom who is aware of the source that has made my second turn at night cops reporter occasionally satisfying. And Sally can keep a secret.

I shake my head.

"Higher?"

I tap her desk twice and walk away.

I can pull my punches and still give the readers enough to keep any more of them from canceling their subscriptions.

Sarah Goodnight is making herself some hot tea when I go into the break room. I ask her how the story on fearful young women in the city is coming along.

"Lot of jumpy out there," Sarah says, taking a sip as I pour some of our office sludge into my cup, which is older than she is. "Probably wouldn't have been a good idea to send a guy on this one. Might have gotten his ass pepper-sprayed."

It cracks me up and kind of breaks me up to see our young reporters work so hard to be tough and cynical. Dropping subjects and verbs from the front of sentences and speaking out of the corner of your mouth is part of it. It is almost a form of self-mutilation, and I think the young women do it more than the men do, probably because they're afraid we won't think they're tough enough if they hang on to a shard of their innocence. Maybe it will change when women rule the newsroom. Looking around at who does the work around here, I think that day ought to get here about Thursday.

Sarah will have a story for tomorrow on the Tweety Bird scare.

"You know what's really sick?" she asks me as we walk back to her desk. "Somebody's hawking Tweety Bird T-shirts over on Grace Street, right next to the VCU campus. And they're selling. Here, I bought one. Thought I'd turn it in as a business expense."

She takes the tee from her desk and hands it to me. On the front is a wide-eyed, vaguely feminine Tweety Bird. Underneath is the old cartoon line: "I tawt I taw a puddy tat."

I can tell that Sarah thinks this will make me laugh, or at least smile. When I tell her that I visited the late Kelli Jonas's parents two days ago, she puts the shirt away.

"Yeah," she says, giving me a rueful smile, "we are a bunch of assholes, aren't we?"

I don't know if she means the whole human race or just newspaper people, but in either case, I'm in no mood to argue the point.

WHILE I'M WORKING on my story, Wheelie comes down. He moves into the open space in the middle of the newsroom, a vast prairie sprouting tumbleweeds where now-departed reporters and editors labored not too long ago.

He begs our attention. When we gather around, he introduces the rather attractive, late-forties vintage woman at his side.

After a few mumbled introductory pleasantries about doing more with less, during which I am afraid Enos Jackson or one of the other hard-ridden veteran editors is going to attack him with a pica pole, he introduces our new publisher.

Her name is Rita Dominick. She is a blonde, at least for the moment. She has one of those cuts like that woman on *House of Cards*. It must be the in thing. Sally said she saw a fat, unattractive woman come into the hair salon, pull out the woman's picture and tell the stylist, "Make me look like that."

Rita Dominick is wearing a red dress that is stylish and does what it is supposed to do: exude the sense that she could kill you in bed or just rip your head off and crap down your neck for fun. I'm guessing she does either yoga or judo and stays away from saturated fats. She was the head of advertising at the only paper in our chain that's larger than us. She's married with two kids, for whom I feel sorry, for some reason.

I'm sure Wheelie's relieved to get back in the newsroom. He'd never been that close to the brimstone before. Ms. Dominick ("Call me Rita") speaks to us about our exciting future. She talks about turning the corner. The only corners we've turned lately have brought us face-to-face with joblessness or salary cuts, so we're a little skeptical. We're pretty much over corners.

I glance at Baer. His head is going up and down like one of those bobblehead dolls they sell at the ballpark. He's eating it up. Another place to put his brownish schnoz.

It just goes to show you. Things can always be worse. You can have a publisher like the late James H. Grubbs, who used his considerable clout to get rid of a large chunk of his former friends and mentors, only to wake up one fine September morning and find out that you are now in the clutches of advertising. Jesus Christ.

Wheelie brings her around and introduces her to as many of us as can't find somewhere else to be. I look up, and she's standing there, looking down at me.

"And this," Wheelie says, a half smile, half grimace on his face indicating to me they've already had a discussion about my merits and demerits, "is Willie Black."

"Ah, yes," my new publisher says, "the famous Willie Black."

It doesn't sound like a compliment.

I GET A call as I'm finishing up my story on Ronnie Sax taking it on the lam.

It's Kate. I ask her how the new baby's doing, but she talks over me.

"Willie," she says "we just got a call. From Ronnie Sax. He wants to talk to you. To us. You and Marcus and me."

Sax took my advice. He called Marcus Green's firm first thing this morning, from a cell phone at an undisclosed location.

"He told us he didn't do any of this," Kate says, "but he's afraid once they get him in jail, it's going to be a *fait accompli*."

"He said '*fait accompli*'?"

"He said they were going to railroad his ass."

I ask Kate if she and Marcus are going to give me a finder's fee for this one.

She has to speak up over a baby yowling in the background.

"I don't know what you've found. From what I'm seeing, he's as good a suspect as any right now. He was living in the Bottom, he has a record and he has a penchant for porn."

I concede that I can't vouch for Ronnie Sax, but I tell her that I wanted to throw a little business Marcus's way, knowing that he would rather be on TV than eat a prime rib at Morton's.

I ask her if she doesn't want to go and comfort her bouncing baby girl, who sounds as if she has a safety pin stuck in her butt.

"Greg!" I hear my ex-wife and landlady shout. "Grace has got a diaper full!"

Nothing like a little bundle of joy to add some romance to young lovers' lives. Kate was a lot of fun, and I still love her, in my half-ass fashion, but I'm wondering if she is going to find total fulfillment in motherhood.

"He didn't tell you where he is?"

"We're supposed to meet him. I can't tell you where, but come here in the morning at seven and we'll take you there."

I wonder out loud if she and Marcus Green aren't skating on thin legal ice.

She says she's considered that. I know Marcus likes to blast right through those warning signs, the ones that say, "Caution: Disbarment Ahead." He's come close a couple of times. But Kate likes to play by the rules.

"Marcus says we're OK," she tells me, lowering her voice as if she doesn't want Mr. Ellis to hear. "He says we're just going to have a meeting with our client, to try and get him to turn himself in."

Sounds a little dicey to me, but I tell her I'll be there. After all, I'm only a journalist. We don't have licenses. If we did, getting yours pulled would be about as devastating as being kicked out of AARP.

CHAPTER SEVEN

Tuesday

I'm at Marcus Green's office at 6:55. Kate seems surprised, perhaps because she's never seen me arrive early for anything, including our wedding. This is one appointment, though, that I don't want to miss. I am fairly certain that I have information that Ronnie Sax's potential legal team does not possess.

Richmond can be a small place, especially if you've lived here your whole life and have had dealings with everyone from the governor to guys like Awesome Dude.

LAST NIGHT I got another call from Cindy Peroni. My hope was that Cindy was calling to tell me she could not live a minute longer without me. That didn't happen, but she did that thing the reporter in me always hopes people will do. She told me something I didn't know already.

"I saw your story in the paper, about the Tweety Bird Killer, and I thought something sounded familiar."

It turns out that one of Cindy's friends in the between-husbands set is Mary Kate Kusack Brown. Mary Kate is two years younger than her brother and, unlike him, never saw fit to change her last name until she got married.

"When I saw that he'd changed his name from Kusack, I knew that was the brother she'd mentioned. I called her. She says she's sure Ronnie didn't do it. She says he wouldn't hurt a fly. She says her girls are crazy about him. She thinks you all ought to leave him alone."

I asked her if she thought Mary Kate might be a tad concerned that her brother has a history of porn-related activities, or that whatever the police found on his computer was enough to send them scurrying back to his apartment, a few hours too late, to arrest him.

I offered the opinion that he wouldn't have been the uncle I'd have sent the girls to for a sleepover.

"Well, Mary Kate says he's a good uncle, and a good brother. She says he's sowed his wild oats, but he's past all that."

I told Cindy that I hope her friend's sisterly intuition is right. If I had been telling her the truth, though, I'd have said I hope he's the one and that they catch him fast. I want to get the son of a bitch who's doing this off the streets. My meeting this morning might be a step in the right direction, although I wonder if I did the right thing in suggesting that he employ Marcus Green. Even if he is guilty, Marcus might get him off. Marcus could have sprung Judas Iscariot.

"There's one other thing," Cindy said, just as I was about to try and steer the conversation in a more romantic direction.

"What?"

"She says he was at her house that Thursday night. She said he didn't leave until after eleven."

So I'm thinking Ronnie Sax at least has someone to back up his alibi, although I've seen more than enough relatives swear that their miscreant son/father/brother was having milk and cookies with them when all evidence put him at the scene of the crime.

Before she hung up, I asked Cindy if she'd like to have dinner with me sometime.

"Maybe," she said, then told me she had another call coming in. I have not yet climbed back high enough in Ms. Peroni's esteem to trump an incoming call. Tomorrow is another day.

The information I have that Marcus and Kate don't possess came from Peachy Love. It probably will soon be in the public domain.

After my interrupted phone call with Cindy, I decided to drop in on Peachy. Maybe I was feeling a little miffed about my failure to get back in Cindy's good graces. Maybe—stop the presses—I was horny.

Peachy was home. It was one of those things where you tell yourself, I don't really want to be bad, and if Peachy is out somewhere, it'll be a sign that I should take Mr. Johnson home.

"Well," she said when she opened the door, glancing both ways to make sure nobody in a police car was nearby, "you did decide to cross the tracks, didn't you?"

We had a good time. We always have a good time. If I were smart, I'd probably try to be more than an occasional lover. But Peachy seems to want it that way, too. She has a guy. He works for the police up in DC, and she says maybe one day they'll move in together. I asked her once if she loved him. She hesitated too long before she answered. It seems sometimes like nobody is ever going to get married again. I have mentioned this, gently I thought, to Andi, who reminded me that, between us, we've been married three times, which probably is enough for right now.

At any rate, my occasional night with Peachy has to end before the sun comes up. If somebody recognizes me doing the walk of shame away from the police flack's house, Peachy might be out of a job.

While we were lying there in the dark, both of us smoking in bed, she told me the thing I now know that Sax's lawyers don't.

When the cops were perusing the photographer's digital porn collection, a face stood out to one of them.

"Turns out," Peachy said, "it was the girl at the station."

"The Caldwell girl."

"Yep. There she was, her or her identical twin, wearing her birthday suit and smiling for the camera and sucking on a pacifier with a stuffed toy between her legs. Trying to look even younger, I guess."

Peachy didn't have to remind me that I didn't get that information from her. I thanked her profusely for it. I didn't mention, for some reason, that I might be talking with Mr. Sax within a couple of hours after I left her warm and welcoming bed. No sense in telling everything.

"Come back anytime," she said as she turned off the porch light and I slipped out the door at four thirty. I said I would. I really meant it.

MARCUS GREEN SHOWS up at 7:05. He's dressed to the nines, as always. Marcus might sleep in a three-piece suit. He glances at my jeans and pullover sweater and remarks that it's too bad I didn't have time to dress.

I advise him to screw himself.

Kate looks lovely, even if you disregard the fact that she's recently given birth. She might weigh less than she did before she got knocked up. Her jeans make a much better impression than mine and elicit no comment from Marcus.

"So," I ask them, "do you have to blindfold me first?"

Marcus doesn't answer, just walks toward his Yukon with us following.

He heads down Franklin Street and around the capitol, and I deduce that we're headed for the Bottom.

It never looks that great in daylight, since many of its finer establishments closed only a few hours ago and won't open again until the afternoon. The broken beer bottles glint in the morning sun like cheap costume jewelry.

Marcus turns left, and we go one block up and two blocks over, finally stopping at one of the many old brick buildings that are being repurposed as overpriced housing. This one probably sat for twenty years before someone saw its potential as something other than a source for old bricks and timbers.

We walk inside one of the buildings and go up to the second floor, where Green knocks four times, then twice. The door opens a crack. We walk inside, and there's our man, Ronnie Sax.

Sax doesn't look like he's slept much. He smells like he hasn't showered in the last day either.

Green asks him whose place this is, and Sax says it belongs to a friend who's out of town.

"I need you to help me," he says.

"Well, that depends on whether you're guilty or not," Marcus says. Actually it depends on whether he thinks he can get Ronnie Sax off and garner some free publicity in the process.

"I ain't guilty of nothing. The cops've had it in for me a long time."

He turns to me.

"You know what I told you," he says. "My sister will vouch for me. She knows where I was that night."

It's probably time to drop a little truth bomb on Mr. Sax.

I tell him, along with Marcus and Kate, what I know, without divulging how I know it, about the images the cops have of the late Jessica Caldwell.

"They're pretty sure they have you nailed for taking pictures of an underage girl, Ronnie, right before somebody raped and murdered her."

"Goddamn," he says after a slight pause. "That was her? Well, maybe I did take pictures of her. But that doesn't mean I killed her, does it?"

I note that, if they were to list everyone in the city of Richmond, he might be Number One on the "most likely" list.

Kate glares at me. Once again I'm guilty of not sharing. Well, hell, I only found it out myself a few hours ago.

"You've got to come clean with us," Marcus says. "I am not going into court looking like a fool. What kind of crap are you trying to hand me?"

I'm about ready to call it a day myself. I'm thinking about a tall tree and a thick rope.

"No. Wait," Sax says as Green starts heading back toward the door we just entered. "I've took pictures of a lot of girls. But there's no way I killed anybody. And my sister will tell you I was at her house the night it happened."

I observe that his sister seems to be one of the few people in the greater Richmond area who believes he's not a serial killer. I further note that sisters have been known to lie to save their brothers' asses. Marcus frowns. He doesn't like it that I seem to be steering the conversation. Marcus likes to be behind the wheel.

"Well," Sax says, "I just thank God she'll come through for me."

"If this goes to court, and she swears that, and it turns out not to be true," Kate says, "that would be perjury. She could go to prison for that."

Sax actually grins, showing his crooked teeth, and gives off that weird, kind of spooky, little laugh, like a rusty hinge squeaking.

"She'll back me up," he says. "She loves me."

I am troubled, and I can see that the two lawyers are, too. We are all figuring the odds. Guy takes nasty pictures of girls and two of them wind up raped and murdered. He doesn't have a record of violence, and he has, for the time being, an alibi. Still I'm starting to think Ronnie Sax might be a good deal less harmless than I was thinking he was.

"Is there some way your sister can prove you were there?" Marcus asks him.

"I'm not sure," he says. "Maybe one of the neighbors saw my car?"

Then he snaps his fingers.

"Yeah! We were out on the back porch, talking. Mary Kate was talking with her next-door neighbors, and she told them she had family visiting. I said hi to them."

I ask if the neighbors saw him.

"I don't think so. There was just one little lamplight out there. But they heard me."

"Well," Marcus says. "That's something."

Ronnie Sax can't account for his comings and goings in the other three Tweety Bird murders, but Marcus says he's not too concerned about that. He just has to establish that Sax was otherwise engaged when little Jessica Caldwell met her demise.

I think all three of us are feeling like we should leave and wash our hands to get the crud of Ronnie Sax off us. Child pornography isn't what you want to list among your hobbies if you're already suspected of murdering young women.

Marcus Green seems to be thinking.

"I'll tell you what," he says finally. "If you turn your sorry ass in, today, I won't call the cops, and I'll be your attorney."

Both Kate and I look at Marcus as if he's lost his mind.

He looks at us and shrugs.

"What the hell," Marcus says. "I'm bored. I always thought I could win just about anything. This'll prove it."

He turns toward Ronnie Sax.

"And, if I lose, nobody will think the worse of me as a lawyer. Perry Damn Mason would have a hard time getting you past a jury."

Sax doesn't like it, but his choices are limited. I imagine he can hear the figurative bloodhounds. The cops are bound to be close behind. Whatever friend this joint belongs to, they'll be checking out all of Ronnie Sax's friends soon, and the jig will truly be up.

He makes the call.

The cops are there in less than ten minutes. They are not thrilled to see Marcus Green already on the case. L.D. Jones himself arrives two minutes after the first squad cars.

He doesn't acknowledge either Green or myself. I suppose L.D. is happy he's able to call that little press conference he meant to hold yesterday morning.

It's not yet nine A.M., and I already have my story for tomorrow.

As we're leaving, Marcus turns to me.

"You aren't going to write that crap about the pictures of the Caldwell girl, are you?"

I tell him I haven't decided yet. He threatens to make me walk back up the hill to the office. I tell him that's one guaranteed way to make sure I tell all. Actually the cops will probably drop that information on everybody with a TV set or Internet access pretty soon.

The sweat stains on Marcus Green's perfectly ironed blue shirt tell me how conflicted His Glibness is about taking this case on. Marcus might not have much of a conscience, but he does hate to lose.

CHAPTER EIGHT

It always concerns me when our doughty police department is absolutely, positively cocksure they have their man. Call me a cynic, but at least three times in the last four years, our finest have been ready to throw away the proverbial key, only to be proven embarrassingly, spectacularly wrong. I would be falsely modest if I didn't take at least a pinch of credit for being justice's handmaiden. I still get an occasional note from Martin Fell. Robert Gatewood doesn't write or call, seeing me for the self-serving newspaper jackal that I am, knowing that his freedom was just a way to get my byline on A1. Richard Slade is another matter. We are long-lost cousins, after all. We've had a beer or two in the last year. And because his mother, Philomena, has a hand in the effort to stop Wat Chenault from turning slave burial grounds into a Walmart parking lot, she wants to talk to me, too. She thinks that our blood is thicker than printers' ink and that she can play the race and family card. She thinks she can get me to use my meager talents for good instead of, as usual, serving myself. My thought is that, if I play my cards right, I can finesse a two-fer.

Do the right thing or make our readers spit their cornflakes? Please, don't make me choose.

At any rate, she called and wants to meet with me on Thursday. I promised to bring along our link, Peggy, whose hookup with an African American saxophone player lo those many years ago means the paper gets to trot me out as that most treasured of newsroom assets: a minority. I might look Greek or Italian to you, but to the folks who count that sort of thing, Willie Mays Black is as African American as his namesake.

In the meantime, there's a story to write (after first, of course, giving the gist of it away for free to our freeloaders in the ether).

Being able to write a first-person account of Ronnie Sax's surrender and (most of) the events leading up to it will definitely put me on A1. I probably can ride this horse for the foreseeable future. *Arrest made in serial slayings/Reporter was there when photographer surrendered.*

Wheelie asks me if we have to mention that Sax used to work for the paper, but he knows the answer to that one. I suspect that he already is getting marching orders from Ms. "Call Me Rita" Dominick, whose background in advertising makes her less squeamish than she should be about holding the paper to a lower standard than the one to which we hold everyone else. Once she's been here a week or two, she'll probably take the gloves off and start giving orders instead of trying the subtle approach.

"OK," Wheelie says with a sigh, "but can you not lead the story with it?"

Fair enough. I don't mention that Sax is an alumnus until the ninth graf.

I'm still somewhere on the other side of skeptical about Mary Kate Kusack Brown and have her on my short list of people to interview.

Sarah stops by to congratulate me. Wheelie wants her to go back and do stories on how relieved the female populace of Richmond is.

I tell her I just hope they have the right guy.

"Is there any reason to think they don't?"

"Nothing but the police department's sterling track record."

"Well," she says, "this one looks like a slam dunk."

How many times, I ask her, have you seen a slam dunk bounce off the rim? Then I tell her to stop using sports metaphors. She asks me what a "track record" is, then. I tell her that's different.

I intend to go home and take a nap. I'm supposed to be in for real in a couple of hours. Before I can get away, though, the phone rings. It's an internal ring. Like a fool, I answer it.

It's Wheelie. He wants to see me. I ask him if it can wait. He says it can't.

He's still packing up the crap he hauled up to the executive floor. Ms. Dominick already has moved some of her stuff in. The place looks a little crowded.

Wheelie doesn't ask me to sit, so I'm optimistic that this will be a short conversation.

"We got the papers this morning," he says. "Wat Chenault is definitely suing us."

Well, I tell Wheelie, suing and getting aren't the same thing. This doesn't seem to mollify him.

"I just wanted you to know, so maybe we can go easy on Top of the Bottom."

I don't think it would be a good idea to tell Wheelie just yet that I'm meeting with Philomena and Richard Slade day after tomorrow. It would just worry him.

I remain as noncommittal as I can.

"We especially don't see any reason to rehash all that stuff with the girl. That's ancient history."

OK, he's probably right about that. One time reminding our readers that Wat Chenault got caught doing the nasty with a teenager probably is enough.

By the time our chat is over and I'm back downstairs, that two hours has shrunk to an hour and a half. Fuck it. Might as well stay here. I miss the days when I could get by on five hours of shut-eye. Back then, "I'll Sleep When I'm Dead" was a life plan instead of a song. "I'll Sleep When I'm Old" is more like it, and I'm feeling ancient today.

But Wheelie's got my brain moving in an unforeseen direction.

It's a slow night, and I do some checking in the electronic morgue. The person I'm looking for would be in her late twenties by now. Wheelie will crap his pants if he knows I'm sniffing along this trail, but it's really just a shot in the dark. Probably won't lead anywhere.

All I want to know is whether a certain young woman is still among the living.

WHEN SARAH COMES back from interviewing potential victims, I walk over to her desk.

"How would you like to do a little scavenger hunt?" I ask her.

She says her plate is pretty full. She knows, though, that I wouldn't intentionally waste her time. She says she thinks she can find a spot over on the side, beside the broccoli.

What I want to know, I tell her, is the whereabouts of one Leigh Adkins. Sarah's smart. She remembers the name right away.

"She's probably living a normal life somewhere," I tell her, "but I'd just like to know."

Sarah's better at database searches and other tricks of the trade that they didn't teach when I was learning journalism.

"Is that all?"

No, I tell her. I also would like to know if one Wat Chenault has had any other unsavory experiences with young girls.

"And, it's got to be just between us." I explain about the lawsuit.

"Yeah, I can see where you might want to keep that one under your hat, and maybe hand the ball to somebody else. Shit. I did the sports thing again, didn't I?"

"No harm, no foul."

I've made her laugh. It's always a pleasure to make a pretty woman laugh, as long as it's not at you.

SINCE I'M SUPPOSED to back off Wat Chenault, that's exactly where my perverse desire to piss people off takes me. I do some reading. Chenault's people gave us a proposal for their plans for the Bottom, and for the first time I go over it line by line instead of speed-reading it. From what I'm reading, I think I might be the first person in the newsroom to actually parse this crap.

There are a lot of ifs and maybes in the Top of the Bottom scheme. There are grandiose plans involving boutiquey shops and mixed-use housing, a bow to building some kind of museum to honor the slaves who are buried in the Bottom. There's even my favorite bullshit vehicle of all, the artist's rendering. In the rendering, happy people of all races are wandering blissfully and peacefully through pedestrian streets lined with brightly colored shops where smiling merchants are handing out balloons and free food samples. There's a Ferris wheel in the background, next to the slavery museum. About the only thing missing is a goddamned unicorn.

What there's not a lot of, though, are hard, cold promises. Reading carefully, you can see that none of this has to be the way it's spelled out if the power that be, Wat Chenault, doesn't think he's making enough money. The phrase "economically viable" appears three times. And I've seen how easy it is for some sharpster to come to town, get sixty condominiums, a parking deck and a fitness center approved, only to come back three years later, pleading poverty, and get it zoned down to 120 apartments with no off-street parking. And, too often, the old building that was going to be converted turns out not to be "economically feasible," and here come the bulldozers. Even if you don't have Wat Chenault's connections, it ain't that hard.

Some of the best things Richmond has going for it are the preservationists. The mossbacks who want the Civil War to be best-two-out-of-three are the same ones who have resisted tearing down beautiful but old and abandoned buildings. What once was decrepit can one day become charming. And yet, there is always somebody with money and/or influence who wants to bring in the wrecking ball.

So I'm thinking it is going to be very hard to stay away from Wat Chenault while all this is going on.

I've got Sarah trying to find Leigh Adkins, but I decide to take a whack at it. I don't get much beyond Google when it comes to armchair sleuthing, but in this case, that's all it takes.

The story I find never made our paper. There wasn't much to it, really.

One of the little Southside weeklies went high-tech and had its stories scanned for the last forty years or so. When I search for Ms. Adkins, I find out that there are a lot of Leigh Adkinses out there. But when I cut it down to her name and her hometown, only two stories pop up.

The first one was of little Leigh being Junior Miss Peanut in a local beauty pageant. There she is, beaming and posing with Mr. Peanut. She looks like she's about twelve. It looks like Mr. Peanut has his hand on her butt.

The second one was dated July of 2002, less than a year after the sudden and spectacular end of Wat Chenault's political career.

"Girl missing" was the headline, halfway down the front page. Leigh Adkins, then in high school, might have run away from home, but she'd been gone for two days when her mother called the local police. It was not, I imagine, the first time young Leigh had run away.

But there was no other story, at least not one that I could Google.

The story had the mother's name and even the street she lived on.

I called. The woman who answered admitted, after a certain amount of apprehension about talking to a reporter, that she was Mrs. Emily Adkins.

As gently as I could, I asked her about Leigh's whereabouts.

There was quiet on the other end of the phone.

Finally, she said, "Do you know where she is?"

I assured her that I did not.

"Well, I don't neither. She just took off. We don't know where she is. She might be dead for all we know."

Her voice breaks a little. I apologize for disturbing her. She says Leigh went out to a dance that night and never came home.

"She was kind of wild," the mother says. "Sometimes she would stay over at a friend's and not tell me. It like to of drove me crazy."

After a second night of no Leigh, her mother turned in a missing-person report.

"Fat lot of good it did," she says. "The cops didn't act like they even wanted to find her."

I ask about the older sister, only to wish I hadn't. Leigh's sister was killed by a hit-and-run driver five years ago.

"It's just me now," Ms. Adkins says. I apologize again for disturbing her and hang up.

One thing leads to another. One thought sets another one to tumbling, and soon they're falling like dominoes.

I'm remembering something I hadn't thought of in years.

It must have been six months after Wat Chenault's fall from grace that I was at the Tobacco Company, having a drink with several other reporters and a few of our fine statesmen.

I asked one of them, who had sponsored a bill or two with Chenault, if he ever heard anything from his former colleague.

"Oh, yeah," the guy said. "He was up here the other day. We had a few over at the Commonwealth Club."

And then the senator shook his head.

"If I was that girl," he told me, "I think I'd consider moving somewhere else."

"Because of the scandal?"

He took a sip of bourbon and laughed.

"Nah. I don't think that town's big enough for her and Wat Chenault. He said he'd like to wring her scrawny neck for what she did to him."

I didn't mention that it seemed like Wat was responsible for most of the "doing," and I forgot the whole conversation after sharing it with a reporter or two.

Now, though, it does make me wonder.

CHAPTER NINE

Wednesday

Andi called me early this morning.

"Something's wrong with Peggy," she said by way of a greeting.

"More than usual?"

My daughter explained further. It seems that my mother is on a hunger strike of sorts. This is strange, because Peggy smokes enough dope to give an anorexic the munchies.

I told Andi I'd be right over.

Awesome Dude is in the living room when I get there, watching the local fluff show that follows the national fluff show on one of the networks. A guy with a banjo, accompanied by two more guys with guitars, is trying to sing.

"I was going to call, Dude," my mother's more-or-less full-time basement dweller says, "but Peggy wouldn't let me."

Obviously, Peggy's granddaughter is less afraid of being evicted than Mr. Dude is.

"She's lost about ten pounds," he says, looking away from the TV for a few seconds. "She don't need to lose any weight."

I go into Peggy's bedroom. Andi's sitting there beside the bed. Peggy has the covers pulled up to her chin.

"Why aren't you eating?" I ask her.

"Traitor!" she yells at Andi. I suggest that my daughter should maybe go outside and keep Awesome company.

I take a good look at my mother's face. I haven't been paying much attention lately. You can see the shrinkage in the way her eyes look larger, a little more sunken in. The word "careworn" seems appropriate.

I ask her what she's trying to prove.

"Ain't trying to prove anything," she says. "I just want everybody to leave me the hell alone."

I observe that people who care about other people aren't really inclined to do that.

I press her a little more about what's made her throw her own little pity party, although I already know.

"I just figured," she said, "that it isn't going to get any better than this. And this sucks."

"Les?"

"What the hell do you think?"

OK, maybe my mom's got a point. Les's death was a blow. Hell, I miss him, and I didn't see him but maybe once a week. For Peggy, it was the closest thing to that rarest of all blessings, unadulterated love, that she's known from the male companions of her life.

But it's been a year and a half.

When I point this out, she says, "Well, I did give it a try. They say wait a year before you make any big decisions after something like this. I gave it an extra six months, just in case."

"It could still get better."

She snorts.

"I can't see how it's going to get good enough to be half as good as it was."

I can't think of anything else, so I play the guilt card.

"How is it going to look," I ask her, "if your great-grandson (we've been aware now for two weeks that it's going to be a boy) has to grow up knowing he never got to meet you because you were too selfish to stick around? How about the stigma you'll leave, the message that it's OK to stop living because things suck?"

She squints up at me, her eyes just above the covers.

"You're mean," she says.

I think of something.

"Remember Natalie Brookins?"

I have to remind her. Natalie Brookins was the little girl with whom I was madly in love in the fifth grade. One day she told me we had to stop talking to each other. Her parents had told her that. They were afraid that little blonde-haired Natalie would somehow get involved with a half-breed like me and despoil the Brookins family name, which included only a couple of convicted felons.

I didn't see how things were going to get much better. I already was feeling the weight of hand-me-down prejudice parents passed on to their kids, my classmates. This seemed to affirm that I would live life as a shunned being, denied not just the love of Natalie Brookins, but of all desirable female creatures. At eleven, this was a heavy load.

It was late spring and warm enough to go to the river after school.

Peggy got a call from work and had to rush home. I had jumped off the Mayo Bridge over the James, intent until I was maybe halfway down in ending it all and making everyone sorry. Somebody saw it and called the cops. By the time they got there, I had managed to drag myself out of the water, having decided life without Natalie Brookins wasn't the worst thing in the world. Still, they insisted in making a big deal out of it, including calling Peggy at work.

She didn't say much until we got home. I figured she was going to whip my ass. Instead she sat me down at the dining room table. She pulled up a chair and got face-to-face with me. She asked me why. I told her.

She said she was going to have a chat with the "river-rat, white-trash" Brookinses. I begged her not to, and I don't know if she ever did or not.

"In the meantime, though," she said, reaching forward and grabbing me by the collar with both hands and pulling my face within inches of hers, "don't you ever do anything like this again. Don't you dare throw away even a minute of your life. You never know when something special is just around the corner. There will be better days ahead, I promise you."

"Plus," she said, "if you ever try anything like that again, I'll kill you."

I thought it was ill-advised to point out how self-defeating it would be to thwart a would-be suicide by killing him.

"So," I tell Peggy, "I'm telling you just like you told me: you will have better days, I promise you.

"And if you don't eat some goddamned food and stop whining, I'm going to kill you."

I can hear her laugh, albeit involuntarily, under the sheet.

"Just do this," I tell her. "Give it six more months. Wait 'til the baby is born and see if things don't get better."

Peggy says she thinks this is a bunch of bullshit. She does, however, get out of bed. She promises that she will start eating again, even if she doesn't want to. She promises me she will give life a six-month extension.

I advise her to smoke more dope.

Doctor Willie's work here is done.

I HAVE ARRANGED a meeting with Jessica Caldwell's mother at noon. She refused to speak with Baer. One of the small perks of writing for the local paper for more than three decades is that people know you. That, of course, can be a mixed blessing. In this case, though, Maria Caldwell told Baer she would only talk to "that Willie Black fella." She said she thinks I am a "square shooter." Baer seems offended that his shooting isn't so respected. I tell him that it's probably just his accent.

I drop by the newsroom first. It is, I am soon informed by several of my colleagues, another red-letter day for the paper.

Yesterday was the day Ray Long decided he'd had enough. Ray's been on the copy desk forever. It is not a happy place to be.

The first thing newspapers did, when it became apparent that the Internet was going to swallow us whole, was to start cutting bureaus. Check out any state government body, check out Our Nation's Capital, and you'll find a fraction of the reporters keeping an eye on the politicians and other rogues as were there twenty years ago. The henhouse has been left to the foxes.

The second thing to go was copy editing. I can understand, I guess. If you choose between having somebody cover city government and an editor to turn what they write into English, content has the trump card.

The last straw for Ray was when they cut his hours from forty to twenty-eight, just few enough so that his fifty-four-year-old ass wouldn't have health insurance anymore. I can relate: Ray and I both are too old to be attractive additions to anybody else's newsroom staff and too young to die.

So when Ray came in last night, on one of his four seven-hour workdays, he took matters into his own hands. Somebody else might have used a bit more imagination, once he realized that there wasn't one other set of eyes between his tired, heavy-lidded peepers and the guy who picks it up out of the gutter and takes it into the breakfast nook the next morning.

Somebody else might have fabricated some bogus story in which the new publisher has Nazi roots or Wheelie gets caught screwing a male sheep in the newsroom.

What Ray did was elegant in its simplicity. I think Hemingway, who hated adjectives and big words, would have been proud.

Needing one more story to fill up A4, where we cram most everything that happens outside the greater metropolitan area, he eschewed picking off a wire story from Kyrgyzstan or Upper Volta.

Instead, Ray went DIY on us. The headline on the eight-inch prizewinner he created read, "Fuckfuckfuck/fuckfuckfuck." The copy was more of the same, with the fuck word appearing 358 times, with occasional paragraph breaks. The byline: By Fuckfuckfuck/Staff writer.

As Ray knew it would, the paper made it outside the building with his story unscathed. What he hadn't counted on was that one of our pressmen actually decided to read the damn paper. Our printing plant is twenty minutes away from the newsroom, thereby ensuring that we don't have actual warm-off-the-presses copies of tomorrow's editions delivered to the newsroom, the way we used to when the presses were right here in the building.

But this one pressman was going through the A section when he saw something he didn't normally see in our paper, which draws the profanity line somewhere between "sucks" and "frigging."

He called the newsroom. Sally Velez was the only one left, and she probably said the same word that comprised Ray Long's last journalistic offering. Then she did the thing that all editors love to do. She told the sharp-eyed pressman to stop the presses. Then she had whoever was in charge out there call all the trucks, some of them halfway to Charlottesville by then, and tell the drivers to come back to Richmond. Most of them did, but these guys and gals usually have a second day job, and they don't have all night to help us clean up our mess.

And so, we figure about 10,000 readers got the F-word special this morning. The circulation department is not having a good day. Neither is Wheelie or Ms. Dominick, our new publisher. This probably ensures that the rest of us aren't going to have a good day either. This stuff always travels downhill.

Still, though, you have to admire Ray Long's spirit. He cleaned out whatever he planned to take with him before he wrote the fuck story and walked out with it in a grocery bag. I guess he'll pay a visit to HR sometime soon.

They're taking up a collection, very much on the down low. I make a note to treat him to a beer or three sometime soon.

It seems like a good day not to piss anybody off. I slip away before anyone of the management variety sees me.

JESSICA CALDWELL'S MOTHER has red hair, like her late daughter. She lives out in the West End, but not the ritzy part. She answers the door in a bathrobe. She looks as if she hasn't slept for the past week. I want to tell her I can relate, having a daughter and all, but it seems like it would just be piling on to remind her that some people's daughters were not murdered by a monster last week.

Jessica Caldwell had been something of a problem, her mother says. The track record she relates to me sounds a lot like that of the disappeared Leigh Adkins. Got kicked out of public school. Was sent to an expensive private school that cost all that Lucy Caldwell and her second husband could scrape together. Got kicked out of that school for drugs. Went to live with Mrs. Caldwell's first husband, Jessica's father, and his wife. I can only imagine how thrilled the first husband's second wife must have been about that.

"They didn't keep an eye on her like they should have," Lucy Caldwell says, "but Bobby—that's my husband—he kind of said I had to make a choice."

I can see on her face, one that has aged about ten years since last Thursday, that she will be regretting that decision for the rest of her life. She might not have had any better chance of reining in her wild daughter than her first husband did, but she'll always think she could have. I would not like to be Bobby between now and the time he moves out.

I silently thank my stars for Glenn Walker, who married Jeanette after I blew up my first marriage and never treated Andi as anything but his own.

I ask Lucy, as gently as I can, about her daughter's movements in the day or so leading up to last Thursday.

"She called me on Wednesday morning," she says. "She said she was staying with some friends that had a place down in the Bottom. I asked her if she was working on her GED. She said she was, but I don't know."

Lucy Caldwell sits down.

"She was so young. She was a smart girl, but after her father left, she just kind of went wild. I had to work, and she didn't have anybody to ride herd on her."

I don't know how to broach the subject of Ronnie Sax and his camera. There isn't any good way. I mention that the guy they have locked up was a photographer, and that he sometimes used local girls as models.

She gets my drift.

"Oh my God. That son of a bitch. That son of a bitch!"

I assure her that I don't know anything that would suggest that Jessica was posing for him, although Peachy has told me enough to make me sure that the police will be coming by soon with images of her underage daughter that were gleaned from Ronnie Sax's perverted files.

I ask her if she remembered the names of Jessica's friends down in the Bottom. She said her daughter never mentioned their names. I'm wondering if her "friends" won't turn out to be just the one, a lizard by the name of Ronnie Sax. From what Peachy told me, she certainly knew the way to Sax's apartment.

There isn't much left to ask her. On the way out the door, I think to ask her about the tattoo.

"I didn't know anything about that until they brought me down there to see . . ."

I wait a moment for Lucy Caldwell to regain control of what's left of her sense.

"She never would have gotten one, on her own. She didn't like them. She said she didn't want anything that made her hurt . . ."

I let myself out, feeling like almost as big a creep as Ronnie Sax. He wanted to exploit Jessica Caldwell to make a few bucks. I'm using her mother for an A1 byline.

Well, I tell myself as I light up, I at least owe Lucy Caldwell a proper resolution to all this.

I know that's the cops' job, but I just want to make sure they do it right. Ronnie Sax is a vile pornographer who preys on young women. Check. He deserves to spend an appreciable amount of time in the kind of prison where guys like Ronnie get a little payback, in kind. Check.

Is Ronnie Sax the kind of man who brutally murders young women on a regular basis? The cops are no doubt sure of that by now.

Me, I'm never sure 'til I'm sure.

CHAPTER TEN

Thursday

The "We got him" press conference is at nine thirty. I swear L.D. Jones plans these things so he can ensure that every TV station around gets the story before the paper does. That, and it ensures that I will put in a fourteen-hour shift. No big deal, though. We've run pretty much everything worth knowing already. And he's not lengthening my day that much anyhow, because I'm meeting Philomena and Richard Slade for lunch at noon. I'll just have time to listen to some bullshit, write it up for the website and head out to the Slades' place.

Jones and the mayor are looking somber and proud, ebony and ivory back in harmony now that the bad guy's been caught and there are no bucks to pass. They explain that they have strong reason to believe that the person they have in custody is the man responsible for the rape and murder of Jessica Caldwell. They are, the chief adds, also looking into the possible connection to three earlier murders. Then he names the other victims.

He goes on to compliment the anonymous citizen who gave the police the tip they needed. He praises the dogged detective work, not mentioning that they had the guy in custody and then let him go, or that Sax turned himself in.

Someone who must be from out of town or another planet asks him the guy's name. I see the other TV types roll their eyes. When these guys notice your ass is clueless, you're in trouble. Everything I've written so far about this case has turned up on the next TV news cycle, more or less verbatim, including, of course, the alleged perp's name. But the chief, in his giddiness, has forgotten to give us that important detail.

"His name is Ronald Wayne Kusack," Jones says. "He's forty-eight years old. He has been going by the name Ronnie Sax. He worked as a freelance photographer."

L.D. can't resist adding that Sax worked for my newspaper, something that everybody in town already knows.

The chief gives us a few more useless details, and the dog-and-pony show ends. I stop by the paper and file for the ether, using the phrase "as previously reported" as often as I can.

But at least they have the guy. Some wag has found a photo of Sax in his journalism days and has posted it on the newsroom bulletin board. Underneath, someone's written, "Single hot guy ISO female companionship. Must be open-minded. Age no barrier."

Normally I have a fairly sick sense of humor. Thinking of Andi, though, I rip the photo and caption off the wall, crumple them up and dump them in the trash can. Nobody tries to stop me.

I RUN BACK to the Prestwould long enough to pick up the mail. Then it's a two-smoke drive out to the Slades' home. When I get there, I can see Richard's influence. Philomena is a fastidious person, but she's also one old woman who was trying to keep up a house and yard by herself. Richard's been out of prison for more than two years now, released after spending his adult life to that point behind bars.

He seems to have thrown himself into home improvement with the fervor of someone trying to make up for lost time. The yard is as green as an Augusta fairway, even after the Richmond summer that incinerates less-cared-for lawns.

Rose bushes bloom. Other plants I can't name, but look pretty, abound. The smell of mulch hangs in the air. The house itself looks as if it has been painted so recently I should be careful not to touch anything. The roof is new. The state did give Richard Slade a pittance for the oopsie of sending him to prison for twenty-eight years for a crime he didn't commit, and he seems to have spent a goodly sum of it fixing up the home of the one person who never thought he was guilty. He told me, six months after his release, that he had offered to move his mother into a new and larger house, but she refused.

"She said this was the only house she ever needed," he told me at the time.

Since my reporting helped keep Richard from being thrown back into prison, which would have set some kind of record for injustice inflicted on one innocent man, I am treated with more kindness than I deserve. Hell, I was just trying to make A1. It doesn't hurt that the Slades are my cousins.

He shakes my hand and gives me a man-hug. Philomena graces me with a kiss on the cheek.

"Willie Black!" she says. "Our salvation."

I feel myself blushing. I have done much to blush for, but I seldom do.

I compliment Richard and Philomena, suggesting that perhaps they will be on the city's annual home and garden tour.

Philomena tells me to stop lying. I can see she's pleased.

We have lunch and catch up. I give them the short version of Peggy's depression. Philomena promises to come visit her soon and chastises me for not bringing her today. Peggy begged off at the last minute, but I should have dragged her over anyhow.

Over banana pudding, Richard cuts to the chase.

"We wanted to see if you could help us," he says. "It's about what they're doing in the Bottom."

I knew this was where we were headed. I've just been waiting for us to work through the pleasantries.

"What they want to do is wrong," Philomena says. She is a woman of strong convictions and few words. But I know she will go at this like a pit bull with heat rash. Richard and I both know what Philomena Slade will do when she thinks justice is being disrespected.

She has become part of the group that is trying to stave off Wat Chenault's Top of the Bottom plans. The group calls itself Stop the Top. Maybe Philomena volunteered that she knew somebody who could get them some ink.

"My grandmother used to tell me what her grandmother told her, and it was passed down before that, I'm sure, about how terrible it was back then. One of them, I think it was that older grannie's mother, saw two of her children sold there, sold down south somewhere. Never saw them again."

I know oral histories can have more staying power than might seem possible. Philomena, though, has taken it a bit further. What her grandmother told her going back another three generations, Momma Phil wrote down.

"Some others had things, too, that they wrote down that was told to them," she says. "We want to get some of that into your paper."

I tell them I will do what I can. They take this as less than an ironclad promise. I feel bad about that, but the next thing I write speaking ill of Wat Chenault's plans could be the last thing I write for the only place I know that will let me stay in Richmond, do honest work and pay the rent. This is going to take either some fancy dancing or the kind of courage I had more of at twenty-three than I do at fifty-three. The newborn lamb blah-blah-blah.

The school bus pulls up outside and Jamal and Jeroy come bounding to the house. Philomena's keeping them after school while Chanelle, her niece, works. If it takes a village, Momma Phil is certainly this burg's mayor.

"First grade," she says, "and they already can read so good."

They whine for some quality time with Uncle Richard, who obliges them.

"I wish he could find a good woman," Philomena says, as he leads them over to the sawed-off basketball goal. "He's so good with children."

I depart, promising her I will do what I possibly can.

"I know you will," she says. It is good when people have faith in you, but it's bad when you puncture that faith. I know. I have been there. Just ask my former wives.

I TAKE THE mail inside with me when I get back to the paper. Along with a couple of bills, two pieces of correspondence bear the imprint of my alma mater, neither of them asking me to speak at commencement. One is offering me an unbeatable deal on life insurance. The other is promising me the vacation of a lifetime in southern Italy and Sicily, spent with fellow alums, for about a month's pay. Does my old school do anything anymore, education-wise, or is it just in the business of selling my name to as many people as possible? Well, yes, one other thing: It's also good at cashing those checks for Andi's education.

The one piece of mail that looks like it could be from an actual human being wishing to communicate with me has no return address.

Most of the mail I get from readers, I get at the office. It is more likely to start off with "Dear Shithead" than "Dear Willie." It's rare, these days, to receive personal correspondence at home.

I open it. The lined notebook paper inside does not give me hope, nor does the shaky cursive script.

However, the content definitely gets my attention.

"You people," it starts by way of salutation, "you think your so fucking smart. Think you got the right guy, huh?

Well, then, how come I'm writing you, and it's not coming from the Richmond jail?"

This is a very good question.

Of course, anyone could write a note like this. What follows, though, does make me wonder.

"Did the cops look in their pockets?" the letter continues. "Have the cops spent those silver dollars yet? Maybe you ought to check, dumbass."

Not surprisingly, the letter isn't signed. I find out later that it was mailed at the main post office branch on the North Side.

I wait until after six to give Peachy Love a call at home.

"Tell me about the silver dollars," is my greeting.

Peachy is silent for a few seconds.

"OK," she says at last, "but you can't let anyone know you know about this. I think they're a little suspicious around here. The chief called me in yesterday and asked me if I ever talk to 'that asshole at the paper.' Of course, I knew who he meant, but I played dumb. He said your name, and I told him the only time we talk is when you're over here sniffing around or it's a press conference or something like that.

"I'm not sure he believes me."

I assure her that the most I will do is show the cops the letter. Peachy then tells me what I need to know.

In each of the murdered girls' clothing, someone had left a silver dollar. The police had kept that bit of information secret, a way to separate the real killer from idiots who feel compelled to confess to crimes they didn't commit. No one, real or otherwise, came forward until they nabbed Ronnie Sax, and the secret of the silver dollars did what secrets almost never do: It stayed secret. I've always known, in my heart of hearts, that Peachy doesn't tell me everything she knows. I don't guess I'd respect her if she did.

"He really mentioned silver dollars?" Peachy asked.

"Yeah. Do you think it's possible you've got the wrong guy?"

"I've never seen a more perfect perp. He's got a history with girls and young women. He lives in the neighborhood. He had pictures of those two girls on his computer."

I point out that Ronnie Sax has no history of violence, and that no one can place him at or near the train station around the time of the murder.

Sax looks like a natural. I was pretty much ready to pull the switch myself. Now, with the letter, I'm not so sure.

ABOUT NINE, WAT Chenault calls.

"I understand you've got that big nose of yours stuck in my business again," is his idea of a cordial greeting.

I tell him that, with the lawsuit and all, I am proscribed from talking to him.

"Proscribed? Where did an Oregon Hill mulatto like you learn such big words, Willie?"

I resist the urge to either tell him to go fuck himself or pay him a visit and give him an up-close and personal greeting. I grind my teeth and wait.

"I know you've met with that Slade woman," Chenault says. "I know what her and those other colored—excuse me, African American—women are up to. Well, it ain't going to work, and if I see even a hint that you might be siding with her, my lawyer will be paying your new publisher a call. You get me?"

I've gotten Wat Chenault for a long time. What he doesn't get about me, though, is this: If he pisses me off enough, all the lawyers and lawsuits and threats of termination in the world won't keep me quiet.

"I know you and the Slades are family, sort of," he says, chuckling. God, I want to ram his teeth down his fat-ass throat, "but sometimes, you just have to look out for yourself."

I hang up without exchanging further pleasantries, and he doesn't call back.

There is now just about zero chance that Philomena Slade's side of the story won't see the light of day. The only question is how.

I walk over and ask Sarah Goodnight if she's had any luck tracking down the missing Leigh Adkins.

"I haven't had much time, Willie," she says. "Wheelie's got me working on a three-part series on the economic advantages of developing the Bottom. I think it's bullshit, but they do have some impressive numbers."

Numbers. You can lead your average journalist off a cliff with numbers. We're all liberal arts majors, and most of us don't know how many millions in a billion. I'm sure Chenault has some experts working on Sarah. Before you know it, they have you believing that every nineteen-dollar blouse you buy at Walmart brings $200 into the community.

I tell Sarah to be careful, that numbers do lie.

"I know," she says, giving me a look that tells me I've slipped into preachy parent mode, something nobody wants. "I'm not an idiot."

I can't resist.

"How many millions in a billion?"

She asks me what that's got to do with anything. I thank her for any help she can provide and walk away.

An hour later, she comes by. She's checked every online source she can find. There's no sign of Leigh Adkins anywhere.

"Of course," she says, "she could've gotten married, changed her name, whatever. I'll keep checking. Maybe she doesn't want her mother to find her."

I concede that this is possible. I don't think it's probable, but the improbable happens all the time.

I ask Sarah if she thinks Wheelie would be amenable to a sidebar to the first part of her series, one from the point of view of African Americans who don't think paving over their slave ancestors' graves would be such a good idea.

She's quiet for a minute.

"I don't know, Willie. Wheelie says we've written too much already about that side of the story. He wants this one to be about 'positive' stuff."

I tell her that positive is in the eye of the beholder. I, for instance, am positive that Wat Chenault is a grade-A asshole whose full story needs to be told.

I am worried about Sarah. I know our new publisher had a chat with her a couple of days ago. Sarah said Ms. Dominick told her she had a great future in this business, and that she ought to go to school at night and get her MBA.

I did not outright discourage this, and only mentioned the newspaper people we knew who had done this, and what became of them, soul-wise.

"I know, Willie," she said. "I know. But what am I supposed to do? I love newspapers. I want to be here when they come roaring back. I want to be part of the solution."

That sounds like publisher talk to me, but who am I to argue? Am I going to be able to step in when Sarah Goodnight gets laid off just because the fourth-floor bonuses aren't high enough this quarter? Hell, I can barely look out for myself.

"Oh, yeah," she says as she starts to walk away. "It's a thousand."

"Excuse me?"

"Millions in a billion. There are a thousand of them."

Maybe there's hope after all. Nah, she probably just Googled it.

CHAPTER ELEVEN

Friday

Andi is sitting on the porch outside when I get to Peggy's place. She looks like she's been crying.

She phoned me this morning. My daughter doesn't call very often. When she does, she has my attention.

"It's about Quip," she said. I told her I'd be there in a flash, as soon as I woke up and grabbed some clothes.

I walk up onto the porch and sit in the chair beside Andi's. I find we do better heart-to-hearts if we're not looking at each other, for some reason.

I wait.

"He wants me to marry him," she says at last.

Silly me. I think that's good news. No, it turns out. That's bad. Congratulations do not appear to be in order.

"I don't want to marry him," Andi says. "He says he wants to give our baby a name."

"He'll have a name. They won't let you leave the hospital if he doesn't have a name."

I don't know if that's true or not. I do know that, as opposed to 1960, when I was born *sans* dad, there isn't much downside to not having a proud papa around. Must be hell on the cigar business.

I'm no fan of Thomas Jefferson Blandford V, but I note to Andi that there must have been something appealing about the young man, since she chose to live with him for a couple of years.

"He's OK," my daughter says. "But he's not responsible. He won't be good at parenting. I just know it.

"Plus, I don't love him."

It kind of warms my heart to hear my flinty, hard-as-nails daughter talk of love, even in the negative. It takes willpower, though, to keep from asking her if she couldn't at least give it a try. Surely Peggy has given her a primer on the hard road facing a single mother, even in this enlightened century. Surely even a feckless Quip Blandford would be better than nothing at all.

I ask about this.

"Peggy said I'd be better off on my own than with somebody I didn't really care about. Some 'scumbag,' I think is how she put it."

Great, I'm thinking. Thanks, Mom. Guess you figure on having your granddaughter and great-grandson as permanent houseguests.

I ask Andi what Quip said when she turned down his chance at three o'clock feedings and dirty diapers.

"He got mad. He said he was going to make sure he was part of his baby's life, even if he had to hire a lawyer to do it."

I am sure young Quip, or rather his well-heeled daddy, can afford all the lawyers it would take. I make a mental note to talk to the little shithead, something Andi makes me promise not to do.

"If you beat him up," she says, "I'll kill you."

"So why am I here?"

"I dunno," she says, actually extending one of her hands in my direction. Normally, daughterly shows of affection by Andi are about as common as my ordering a club soda at Penny Lane. "I guess I just wanted to talk about it with you."

I am proud of her, actually, for being the strong woman she's growing up to be. She knows what she wants. She isn't afraid of taking the rocky road of single parenthood to get there. And she's smart enough to know a bad husband could be worse than no husband at all. Still I'm not sure she knows what she's signing on for.

Maybe, I suggest, the three of us could talk.

"It won't work," Andi says. "He thinks I'll be raising the baby in some slum. He said he didn't want his son to be raised like white trash."

I silently wonder whether Quip knows that his soon-to-be son's great-grandfather was African American. In Quip's world, that might be enough to quash any hopes of bringing my grandson up in West End affluence, although the blue bloods, or at least the ones who can see the multihued future, are getting more open-minded.

I assure her that, as the mother, she is holding all the high cards. I do worry about Quip, though. If money talks, his father's assets could put on quite a damn filibuster.

I promise her that I'll see what I can do. I further promise that I will do that without busting young Quip's skull. It is a promise I hope I can keep.

I check in on Peggy, who seems to be a little better, mental health-wise.

I should chastise her for advising her granddaughter to forgo marrying a rich man who can afford to double-team her upcoming baby with nannies.

I'm not sure, though, that Peggy isn't right.

After all, look how well I turned out.

L.D. JONES IS in his office. He's busy, his secretary says, after she's told him who's calling. When I tell her that I'm there to ask about the silver dollars, he gets un-busy.

"You better not be bullshitting me," he says. I produce a copy of the letter. He reads it. I can see his lips moving.

"Why," he asks me, slamming the letter down on his desk, "are you causing me so much trouble?"

"I didn't write the letter. I didn't ask anybody to send me a letter. I don't even know why whoever sent it sent it to me."

"They did it because you're the nosiest son of a bitch in Richmond! Why the hell wouldn't they send it to you? Short of hiring a skywriter, how could they get the word out any better?"

"All I need to know from you is if it's true. Did those girls have silver dollars on them?"

The chief says he can't tell me that. I tell him that I don't intend to run this particular bit of information right now, but that I am retaining my right to do so at a later date. But if I don't get confirmation from him, I will put something in the paper about it tomorrow. I don't mention the fact that Kate and the publicity-addicted Marcus Green soon also will be made aware of the letter's presence.

"Just nod if it's true," I say, making it easy on our beleaguered chief.

He glares, and then he nods.

I also ask L.D. if he doesn't think that this might, just maybe, sprinkle a light dusting of doubt on Ronnie Sax's guilt.

"Until we have something more convincing to go on than the pencil-scratching of some anonymous jerk, nothing's changed," the chief says.

I tell L.D. he can keep the letter. He thanks me for nothing. You'd think the police would be more appreciative of helpful tips from civilians.

I DO PAY a visit to Marcus Green's office. Kate has a playpen set up in her space. In the playpen is Grace, her six-month-old bundle of joy. I wonder if whatever bar or eatery Andi's working at half a year from now will be so child-friendly.

Marcus comes out of his office. He frowns toward the playpen where Grace is on all fours, gurgling and looking up at us like we're the most amazing things she's ever seen. I can tell that Marcus has had to decide between bending the rules and keeping the best lawyer he's ever going to get for what he's paying. Still he can't resist kneeling and letting Grace wrap her tiny hand around his finger.

They react favorably to the letter.

Kate starts to ask me why I didn't share this with her earlier. I cut her off by telling her to look at the postmark. Mailed two days ago.

"It just came in yesterday. I rushed right over."

Kate notes that one day later isn't rushing, but she's somewhat appeased.

"Damn," Marcus says. "Maybe the little bastard didn't do it."

"You mean you ever doubted your client's innocence?"

Marcus's facial expression silently asks me if I was born yesterday.

"And this crap about the silver dollars? That's true?"

I assure him that it is.

He and Kate both thank me for the good news.

I tell them I'm not going to write about it, at least not right now. However, I'm sure Marcus will use it to make his case for bail for Ronnie Sax.

IT IS HARD to keep a secret in a newsroom, even one as decimated as ours. By the time I show up for work, the usual air of upheaval is in the wind: clusters of people speaking in muted tones, glancing occasionally at Wheelie's office, where two men in suits sit with their backs to us.

"Who is it this time?" I ask Sally.

"Goddamned Friedman."

"Friedman? No shit?"

"No shit."

We've been aware for some time that we might be sold. What once was a family paper became a chain, even before I signed on. That old feeling that we were protected retainers of our familial guardians, safe from the ravages of corporate

America, took wing a long time ago, along with pensions, matching 401(k) funds, and job security.

And then, some genius upstairs thought it would be a good idea to buy six more newspapers in various parts of the South with borrowed money. In 2007. Just before the crash. If you took out a home mortgage about that time with 10 percent down, you might be able to guess what happened.

Long story short, the bank has us by the short ones. And corporate keeps throwing pieces of our enterprise overboard, hoping what's left of our tempest-tossed vessel eventually will be light enough to float again. One of the pieces being prepped for cement overshoes is our paper. At least three other chains have had people snooping around here, kicking the tires.

But Friedman? Jesus. Those guys have ruined four good newspapers that I know of. They never saw a newsroom they couldn't shrink. The rule of thumb for the print peons always has been one of us for every 1,000 circulation. So it becomes a self-fulfilling prophecy: Every time circulation drops another grand because we're more or less giving it away online, a reporter, photographer, designer or editor bites the dust. (HR seems immune from this somehow.) The paper gets a little thinner, and more people drop their subscriptions, so we cut more, ad nauseam.

"The perfect paper," Enos Jackson once said after a few bourbons, "would be one staffer and one reader. Hardly any overhead at all."

We're headed that way, and if Friedman buys us, that will grease the skids. One of their papers, in a college town two states away, made a deal with the journalism department to let their kids cover city council and the school board as part of their course. Will work for grades. Great experience for the kids. Not so great for the readers.

I'm not presenting myself as a knight in shining armor, giving all for the public good. Like so many of my coworkers, I'm just a busybody who loves getting paid to snoop. Most of our readers, I'd just as soon not break bread with them. But if we don't keep an eye on the thieves and idiots, who the hell will?

"You'll miss us when we're gone," I heard Jackson say one time when he was being lambasted by an unhappy reader. Then Jackson laughed and hung up.

I asked him what was so funny.

Jackson looked over at me.

"He said he'd like to have the opportunity."

WAT CHENAULT HAS me in a quandary. I would dearly love to cut his legs out from under him. If I do, though, I might not be able to dig deep enough to really get to the cesspool bottom of all this. I'm not feeling good about Ms. Leigh Adkins.

I have a couple of hours to do a little digging. If this gets back to Chenault, I might be hollowing out a nice little professional grave for myself.

I catch Johnny Grimes by phone before nine, which is always good. After nine, Johnny's not much good for information. By ten, he has trouble speaking in coherent sentences.

He was a great reporter for us once upon a time. We nominated him for Pulitzers twice, and he was a finalist once, but after the *New York* Fucking *Times* got through giving itself three or four and the *Washington Post* got a couple and they threw the obligatory one to some dog-ass weekly that caught the mayor screwing a goat, there weren't any left for Johnny Grimes.

He and I used to drink together. When people tell me I have a drinking problem, I tell them they should have seen Johnny Grimes.

Johnny lost control of the bottle sometime in his thirties, when I was still a pup and viewed him as the epitome of what the hard-boiled newsman should be. Perhaps I can attribute some of my missteps to the fact that I didn't choose the right role models. Johnny missed assignments, once passed out during a city council meeting and was known to fall asleep at his desk. The managing editor finally got so mad at him that he sent him to sports, where bad quickly became worse, abetted by professional drinkers like Bootie Carmichael. Yeah, I was there too, buying rounds and listening to the stories.

They finally let him go, and we assumed he'd turn up in an obit. We tried to keep in touch with him, and he disappeared for a time, taking a job out in Montana, where sobriety standards apparently are a bit less restrictive.

And then, one day, he resurfaced, at the Southside Herald. It's a weekly with about 5,000 circulation and a staff to match. But Johnny's done well there. They tend to overlook the bottle in his desk, because he's far and away the best journalist they've ever had.

"Willie!" he says, shouting into the phone. I can hear a ball game going in the background. "What can I do you for?"

I explain that I need some off-the-record information on a certain real-estate developer. I don't show all my cards, but I do mention that we're being sued after reviving some of Mr. Chenault's sordid history.

"Were there any other incidents like that, maybe stuff you've heard?"

I can hear ice cubes clinking.

"He's not exactly been what you'd call a saint," Johnny says at last. "There's always talk. Town's so damn small you can't fart without somebody smelling it."

"But this would be about girls, probably way below the age of consent."

Johnny tells me about a hushed-up problem with a female student at the local high school where Chenault was helping coach the girls soccer team "that happened before my time here." Why anyone would let Wat Chenault coach a girls' anything team is beyond me.

"And there were rumors that shit like that is what made Mrs. Chenault leave him. But nobody ever brought charges."

"Did any of that involve violence?"

"Not that I know of. But Wat's definitely capable. You really don't want to cross him."

Too late for that.

I get a couple of names. We talk about old times, the way we want to remember them.

"Remember the corn kernels?" Johnny asks. He doesn't have to say anything more, but we take turns telling the story to each other anyhow.

One of our corporate masters, an old Virginia type with more manners than brains, got busted for baiting by the game department. He had spread corn kernels all over an open field the night before he and a bunch of his buddies were going to gather and shoot some doves. The wildlife folks don't consider that to be fair play. The asshole managed to get himself on B2 in Sunday's paper, complete with a mug shot.

On Monday morning, the guy comes into the lobby downstairs and finds kernels of corn leading from the front door to the elevator. He gets off on the top floor, and the trail continues, right to his office. Everyone knew Johnny had done it, but nobody could prove it, and he was still enough of an asset that nobody really wanted to.

Johnny and I laugh a little, but I already can sense the sun of sobriety starting to set on my old compatriot.

He asks me to share with him "in case the publisher down here has the balls to let us print anything about it."

I promise Johnny I'll pay him back. He tells me to come down and help him kill a bottle sometime.

I tell him I will, but we both know I'm lying.

CHAPTER TWELVE

Saturday

I spend a couple of hours over at Ronnie Sax's apartment complex on Tobacco Row. I have an appointment to talk with his alibiing sister tomorrow, but I wanted to get some insight from people who aren't related to him and haven't maybe been lying lately to cover his ass.

Everyone's a little skittish. At first, none of them want to talk about their former neighbor. The cops have already been through, getting any shred of information they can. The residents probably are a little interview-weary.

Finally, though, a couple of guys who live in the apartment below his who are bringing in their groceries let me ask them some questions. They tell me that Sax did occasionally bring women to his unit, "or more like girls, actually."

"He seemed to like them young," one of them tells me. "But, you know, he was a good neighbor. Never made a lot of noise. I can't believe he killed those girls."

About all it takes, apparently, to be a good neighbor around here is to keep the music down.

Neither of them, nor any of the other people I finally manage to waylay, have ever seen Sax go even a little bit postal.

"He was kinda weird, though," one girl said a few minutes later. "He had this funny laugh, kind of, like, braying." She gives a pretty good imitation.

"Whatever he did," she says, "he probably didn't do it here. Too many people."

"Did he ever talk about having another place somewhere?"

The girl says she's heard he has the studio, but I know the cops have combed that thoroughly by now.

"I talked to him a couple of months ago, at a pool party, and I think he mentioned something about going over to a friend's place, but I can't remember where. Never saw him with anybody else around here, except the girls, of course." She gives a little shiver, probably for effect, and excuses herself.

I go by the apartment where Sax turned himself in four days ago. The guy who lives there is back. He said he didn't even know Sax was there. He had been out of town on business for two weeks and didn't know about any of this until he got home and found his place tossed and a couple of cops in an unmarked car waiting to give him a welcome-home party.

"They handcuffed my ass," he says. "I told them I'd just got back into town, but it took them half an hour to believe me."

Sax, it turned out, had been a casual acquaintance of the guy and knew in which flowerpot he hid his house key.

"If they don't fry him," the guy says, "I want a piece of him."

No, the guy didn't know anyone who could qualify as a friend of Ronnie Sax.

"He might've said I was one," he says as he leads me out, "but if I ever was, I sure as hell ain't now."

MY DANCE CARD'S pretty full today. I got a call yesterday from Philomena and promised I'd meet with her and a friend. I have just enough time to go by Buzz and Ned's for some 'cue, run over to the Bottom and get back to the paper by three. I am praying for a quiet night. Tomorrow's the first day of fall, but it still feels like summer, and the higher the temperature, the more likely our gun-toting citizenry is to get all itchy and start plugging each other.

I'm still picking pieces of pulled pork out of my teeth when I find a parking space back behind the Farmers' Market. Philomena and her friend are waiting for me at the market. We find a bench.

"Sophia knows something you ought to be aware of," my cousin says, all business as usual.

The woman appears to be about Philomena's age. I can imagine her offering Momma Phil comfort in those twenty-eight long years when Richard was falsely imprisoned.

"My nephew, he saw it," Sophia says. "They dug up something down there. It was bones."

I am all ears and no mouth. It turns out that Sophia's nephew is in construction. He was driving a bulldozer, doing some preliminary clearing not far from where we're sitting, in the acreage where Top of the Bottom either will or won't be built.

The nephew saw something. He got off his bulldozer, the way he told it to his aunt, and there were bones there.

"He called his supervisor over, and he said the supervisor called somebody, and this big, rough-looking fella was there in maybe fifteen minutes. He told them to cover it up and knock off for the day.

"When my nephew came back the next day, he said it looked like somebody had dug up every bit of dirt in that place, down maybe ten feet, and then brought more dirt back in to fill."

The "big, rough-looking fella" sounds, from Sophia's second-hand description, a lot like my favorite former state senator. The nephew said he looked kind of like a toad frog in a suit.

"You know what those bones were," Philomena says. I have a pretty good idea. They supposedly gave slaves such half-ass burials as they were accorded somewhere down here in the Bottom. The historians and archaeologists have never found the exact spot. Maybe some guy with a bulldozer did.

I ask, knowing the answer already, why the nephew didn't tell somebody else about it.

"He needs that job," Sophia says. "He didn't work for a couple of years after all the construction dried up. His boss told him he'd never work a day again around here if he told anybody."

"He told you."

She looks insulted.

"I'm family," she says. "Of course he told me."

I hazard a guess that he's not likely to repeat that story to anybody who isn't family.

"Maybe not," Sophia says "but now you know. You can do something about it. Just don't mention my nephew."

That's how it goes for your basic buttinsky newsmonger. Everybody has a story, but nobody wants to step up to the plate and be quoted. Not that I blame the nephew. My job is to figure out how, without getting an honest laborer fired, to tell the world that Wat Chenault is covering up the fact that he is, as the preservationists feared, desecrating a slave graveyard.

Hell, if I put this one out there, the nephew and I both will be out of jobs. Maybe we can start a business together, muckraking and backhoeing or some such shit.

But, where there's a Willie, there's a way.

DRIVING BACK TO the paper, I suck on a Camel and try to figure out my next move. I am becoming more and more suspicious of Mr. Chenault, and my suspicions are ranging beyond the area of real-estate scumbaggery and into more serious matters. I'm wondering who sent that letter after Ronnie Sax was locked up, and why.

It occurs to me that I should let this one ride. Maybe I can get either Sarah or Mark Baer to take up the fight, with me feeding them. I don't think Sarah's up for it right now, though. I am afraid she sees an office and a title in her future. And Baer is smart enough to know that the downside of this one probably outweighs the upside. Also, there's the new regime. Even if Wheelie wanted to dabble in Pyrrhic victories, the new publisher is watching us like a hawk. Busting on a guy who's already suing us? Hell, it probably would get red-flagged before it even got into the paper. They've kind of tightened up on the editing process since the Ray Long incident.

There really is only one solution: Feed it to the *Scimitar.*

That's really its name. The *Scimitar* is actually more like a dull, rusty blade, but it does have its following in the African American community, where our paper has a hard-earned reputation for bias. But we're trying to be better. I'd say that, on the sensitivity calendar, we're up to about 1993 now.

Earl Pemberton-Wise, the publisher, used to work for my paper. We were friends and still are, with the cautiousness that comes from being on opposite sides of the fence. Earl tries from time to time to get me to jump ship, trying to make me feel like a race traitor or an Uncle Tom. But when I mention the salary that I would require, he reminds me that he's making about $10,000 less than that himself.

"Ah, the golden handcuffs," he said to me the last time we had this discussion.

I told him it's all I've ever known.

I SLIP INTO the *Scimitar*'s rented digs, four blocks from our paper. Earl is in his office, such as it is. A handful of reporters look at me with suspicion, probably regretting that their rag can't afford security guards. I'm the closest thing to a white guy in their newsroom right now.

"Ready to come to work for a real paper?" Earl says.

I tell him I'm ready to give him something that'll make people buy his Sunday birdcage liner for a change.

I spell it out to him. He's dubious at first. He knows Chenault is already suing us.

I appeal to his pride, asking him if he's going to let some fat white guy from the Southside get away with this crap because he's too afraid to take him on.

"I'm not afraid of anybody in this goddamned town," he says. "Wat Chenault can kiss my ass. The whole damn Commonwealth Club can kiss my ass."

He walks around a bit, talking it out to me and himself.

"Hell, if he sues us, what's he gonna get? And if it's true, we've got nothing to worry about. I mean, he can't prove malice, right?"

I nod my head, helping Earl—who is seeping malice right now—convince himself.

The plan is pretty simple. I feed a slightly fictionalized version of this information—given to me, leaving out the bulldozer driver and his aunt—to one of the *Scimitar*'s reporters, who writes the story under his byline. He isn't likely to tell anybody it isn't his story, since it's probably the best one he's ever going to get.

We have to do some fancy dancing. This story is going to be strong on "a source said," with a lot of the ol' innuendo. In the version that will appear in the *Scimitar*, a kid playing over there found some bones and told his parents about them. The parents have in turn contacted unnamed preservationists. And when the kid went back there, the place had been dug up and replaced with fill dirt.

It's mostly bullshit, of course, but it will get the word out. Hell, my paper might even be able to run with it now, leading off with "as reported in the *Scimitar*," of course. Those words will make Wheelie choke on his coffee, but being the second-hand bearer of bad news doesn't have the same legal peril as going first would.

I have convinced Earl Pemberton-Wise that the better good is being served by letting the city in general know that there probably is a slave graveyard down there in the Bottom, where Wat Chenault wants to build Top of the Bottom, and that some fat redneck came in and did a cover-up.

Earl calls his designated reporter in and explains what we're doing. The reporter is more than a little suspicious, but who wants to turn down a story that everybody else is going to pick up?

This is not my finest hour in journalism, but I'm determined that this story will see the light of day. I'm equally determined not to lose my job for turning the spotlight on it if I can help it.

"Willie," Earl says to me after telling his page designer to tear up A1, "you're sure about this, right?"

"I'm sure there's a slave graveyard down there. I'm sure somebody dug up part of it with a bulldozer. I'm sure somebody who looks a lot like Wat Chenault had the evidence hauled away somewhere."

He sighs.

"Hell," he says, "truth doesn't always come in a neat little package, does it?"

I tell him that he has to keep my name out of it.

"Well," he says, slapping me on the back, "you can always come to work for an honest newspaper."

I convince Earl, before I leave, that the ability to pay my rent and buy food, cigarettes and beer is no laughing matter.

I'm at work half an hour late. Sally Velez mentions this, and I tell her that I've already put in about three good hours in the name of journalism today. I don't mention that our paper isn't going to be the immediate beneficiary of said journalism.

SARAH HASN'T BEEN able to come up with any more information on Leigh Adkins.

"I've looked just about everywhere I know to look," she says. "Nobody seems to know anything about her since she disappeared."

I've done some checking on my own, with equally unsuccessful results. Every source I have on the local and state levels has no trace of Ms. Adkins, and nobody's been looking for her in a very long while.

Johnny Grimes gave me the name of one retired cop in his town who might know more than he does about Wat Chenault's past misdeeds. I catch the guy at home late in the afternoon, but when I start asking him about Wat Chenault, he gets a little antsy. When I push the issue, he tells me to screw myself before he hangs up.

I'm hoping my conversation doesn't get back to Chenault. If it does, though, I have one thing in my favor. I was smart enough to give the ex-cop a fake name and tell him I was from the Norfolk paper.

I am not, evidence notwithstanding, a complete idiot. I'm just hoping the old guy doesn't think to check his phone records.

A COUPLE OF shootings, one a fatality and the other a near miss, spoil my evening. To be honest, though, sitting at the desk playing solitaire and bullshitting with the remnants of our copy desk makes me yearn for some excuse to get out of the office.

On the way back from the fatal shooting, I stop by Havana 59 and see Andi. She looks tired. When I mention that, she takes offense. Now she looks tired and cranky.

If she were to marry Thomas Jefferson Blandford V, I'm pretty sure she could afford to quit this crap, at least until the baby's born.

I respect her for her backbone, but my heart is heavy and I wish I could win the lottery.

CHAPTER THIRTEEN

Sunday

It doesn't take long for the story I planted to take full effect. Not many people read the *Scimitar*. Even fewer get it by home delivery on Sundays. And the leadership of our paper is so far removed from the African American community that a rare newsworthy story in the Sunday morning edition usually wouldn't reach their tone-deaf ears until Monday or Tuesday.

This one, though, grows legs. Earl Pemberton-Wise was smart enough to tip off the local TV stations. With their bare-bones staffs even more emaciated on Sundays, the good-hair folks were happy enough to read this tidbit out of Earl's paper to their viewers. Earl didn't tell them about it in time for what passes as TV news on Sunday morning around here, but three of the stations were awake enough to put it on their websites. Apparently, somebody looks at those things, because I am still enjoying my morning coffee, pondering whether to grace KubaKuba or Millie's with my brunching presence, when the phone rings.

"Did you know anything about this?" Wheelie asks.

I wish him a good morning and ask for elucidation. I try very hard to sound both concerned and puzzled.

Wheelie is caught between a rock and hard place. He can't exactly berate me for getting my ass beaten on a story from which I have been explicitly pulled. At the same time, he suspects that I somehow have had a hand in the latest unflattering chapter of the Wat Chenault saga finding daylight.

I remind Wheelie that I've been warned off anything involving our favorite developer and swear that I would never give aid and comfort to our enemy, the mighty *Scimitar*.

I hear him sigh.

"Well, I guess we've got to do something with it now. So help me, Willie, if I find out you are involved with this crap . . . Rita's going to have a cow."

No doubt. I suggest that perhaps he should have Sarah do our version. I'd kind of like to see my lovely protégée step back from the dark side, i.e., management. A good reporter is a terrible thing to waste.

Wheelie says he thinks our publisher has her working on something else.

"Like a puff piece on Wat Chenault?"

"We call them features, Willie."

I explain to him that Sarah already knows some of what's going on with Mr. Chenault and could hit the ground running.

"Plus, Baer would love to do a nice, frothy feature story."

Baer probably would not, but he'll do whatever they tell him to do. Plus, if Baer gets on Rita Dominick's good side and winds up selling his soul . . . well, hell, he's halfway there already.

"I'll have to call Rita," Wheelie says, "and see if we can switch." He doesn't sound like it's going to be the high point of his morning. Our publisher doesn't know about the *Scimitar* piece, or she'd have lit Wheelie up already. It's funny how this place works. You're encouraged to call everybody by his or her first name, but that doesn't keep them from taking the chain saw to you. "Rita says you're fired" hurts just as much as "Ms. Dominick says you're fired."

I do feel a teensy bit sorry for her, because she'll be the one who has to call Wat Chenault and explain why we have to run the story, seeing as it'll be on every TV station and website in Richmond by sundown. Then I think about her paycheck versus mine. She can handle it.

I MEET KATE and Marcus Green at Marcus's office, which is starting to look more and more like Kate and Marcus's office, what with the crib and baby mobile in the waiting area. I wonder if Greg Ellis, Kate's most recent husband, is doing his share of the parental caregiving. The baby's spending the afternoon with her doting maternal grandparents, who probably thank God every night that their daughter cut her losses, husband-wise, and traded up the second time around.

We're going to talk with the lovely Ronnie Sax. I ride in the back and tell them as much as they need to know about Wat Chenault and the latest obstacle to his pet project. I stop short of letting them know who leaked the story.

"So you let the gotdamn *Scimitar* beat your ass?" Marcus says, obviously pleased. He pounds on the steering wheel and lets loose with that big booming laugh of his.

I tell him that we've been told to back off, for reasons he, as a registered ambulance chaser, can understand.

"Well, Wat Chenault is a racist pig asshole. I hope they put his butt in jail for this."

I note that Chenault hasn't been linked to anything just yet (at least until and if that bulldozer operator steps up and identifies him).

"I guess old Earl Pemberton-hyphen-Wise finally got himself a reporter who can find his ass with both hands," Marcus says.

Kate is giving me the kind of look she used to employ when she suspected I wasn't being completely honest with her, which was often. But she turns around and doesn't say anything.

SAX SEEMS GLAD to see us. He's been in here for five days now, and he looks like he's enjoyed about all of it he can stand. He knows about the letter I got on Thursday, and he wants to know when we're going to get him out of "this shithole."

I want to tell him that I'm far from sure a shithole isn't the best place for him, until we get more evidence to the contrary, but I'd like to not piss him off just yet. As always, I need information.

"Do you have any idea who might be trying to spring you?" I ask him. "Know any psychopaths that might have done this and let you take the fall and then enjoy laughing at us for arresting the wrong guy?"

Sax glares at me and tells me he doesn't know any "goddamned psychopaths," and notes that it seems like everybody in Richmond, "especially your fucking paper," wants to put him away forever.

"They've got it in for me," he adds.

You make it easy, I want to tell him. I do point out that about the only people around who might possibly be interested in his seeing daylight again are a handful of folks (me, maybe Sarah) at my "fucking paper."

"Well," he says, "I hope you do something quick. I don't like the way these guys are looking at me."

Yeah, I'm thinking, guys who molest and murder girls and young women probably have a pretty full social life behind bars.

He claims not to know who his silent Good Samaritan is, and he's sticking with his claim that his sister can attest to his whereabouts that Wednesday night.

On the way back to Marcus's Yukon, I decide it's time to let Kate and Marcus know about my nagging suspicions about Chenault. They seem like they might be on the verge of just bailing on Ronnie Sax, and who could blame them? But the truth is a slippery bastard sometimes, and I want to make sure we've got it wrestled to the ground before we throw the world's most guilty-seeming slimebag to the wolves.

Marcus is silent as I recount my concerns about Chenault, especially our so-far unsuccessful efforts to find the girl who helped ruin his political career twelve years ago. I mention that Chenault, with an office nearby, where he's masterminding his development deal, has been around long enough to do everything that Ronnie Sax is accused of doing.

Kate is less silent, trying to jump in two or three times to ask me why the hell I didn't tell them about this already.

I hold her off until I've finished laying it out for them.

"You're crazy," my ex-wife says when she can finally get a word in edgewise. "You think this guy's been killing girls and young women for twelve years, and he's never been arrested for anything?"

I offer that maybe he hasn't been a serial killer for twelve years, that maybe he just took some kind of turn for the worse the last few years. But, I add, the killings over the last eighteen months do coincide with Chenault's moving his business to the Bottom. He even has an apartment in one of those expensive high-rises overlooking the river downtown, not five minutes away.

"Willie," Marcus says, "are you sure you aren't just going after this guy for personal reasons? I mean, I know he's suing your butt, and I've heard that crap about what he used to call you when you were covering the General Assembly."

I assure Marcus and Kate that I am not holding some kind of grudge against the pig-eyed sack of shit, and that if I were going to decide who killed those girls on the basis of personality, I might actually rather spend time with Wat Chenault than Ronnie Sax. I don't like either one of the sons of bitches, but that isn't what this is about.

I mention the rumors, via Johnny Grimes, in the Southside town where Chenault lives when he's not trying to rape Richmond's landscape and history.

"And, there's the letter."

"He could've had somebody write it for him," Kate says. "Somebody that knew about the silver dollars."

"He could have told them that."

I observe that, whoever it is, he or she is certainly going out of the way to get involved in a major and heinous crime.

"Who cares that much about Ronnie Sax?"

They concede that this would be a small universe. His sister?

"Have you talked to the sister?" I ask Marcus.

"No. We plan to talk with her tomorrow."

"Don't bother. I'm meeting her tonight."

Actually it was a ruse to get myself in the same room with Cindy Peroni. I asked Cindy to set up a meeting of the three of us, at Cindy's place. I haven't set foot inside there since I scotched (bourbon-ed, actually) the best chance I've had in some time to spend the rest of my life with a good woman.

Marcus isn't happy. He accuses me of hindering his investigation. I tell him that, without me, he doesn't have much of an "investigation."

"I'm just an honest reporter, trying to get a story," I tell them. "If you're good, I'll share it with you."

Marcus threatens to take me to Gilpin Court and feed me to the drug dealers. I laugh and tell him they'd have his Yukon stripped for parts before he could get out of there. Marcus, because he's more African American than me (on the outside, anyhow), loves to go all 'hood on me. I like to remind him that he grew up in the suburbs and now resides in stately splendor at a place on River Road with a post-racial lawn jockey out front.

"Well," he says, "just don't do anything to screw up my case."

He drops me at the Prestwould. I grab a bite and a beer, check in on the Redskins, who are in the process of breaking Custalow's heart again, and then head out.

Sarah calls on my cell.

"Thanks a lot," she says.

I tell her she's welcome. She is not pleased as punch to be assigned cleanup duty, telling our readers what most of them already will know about those bones in the Bottom.

"I thought you'd be happy to be doing real journalism again," I tell her.

"I had that damn feature halfway done, and now Baer gets to take it over. And I get to rewrite the fucking *Scimitar*."

She's quiet for a few seconds.

"Wait a minute," she says. "You know that guy, that Earl Washington-Wise."

"Pemberton-Wise."

"Yeah, and you've been trying to get this crap in the paper. And now, we don't have any choice but to run it."

"Just a little serendipity."

"Serendipity, my ass. You can't write it, and I'll bet you're the one that told Wheelie to put me on it."

I exercise my right to remain silent.

"Dammit, Willie. I'm ready for a little stability. Whoever writes this story isn't going to be very popular with Rita Dominick. I need to do something that'll ensure that I'm not Cary Phillips in ten years."

Cary Phillips was a very good reporter. She worked several beats, won lots of state press awards, and then she merged her writing skills and passion for flicks by becoming as good a movie critic as a paper this size could ever want. Then with the last round of layoffs, they sent her packing. Nothing she did wrong; they just eliminated her position. They decided we could get our movie reviews off the AP wire from now on. She was forty-seven, and now she's doing freelance editing, which pays worse than freelance panhandling, and reviewing movies gratis on some damned blog.

I assure Sarah that she will not be Cary Phillips, but in this business, who knows? I do tell her, though, that she will be here longer than our new publisher, if she chooses to be. I'm pretty sure about that one. I've seen Rita Dominick's type before. They're already angling for the next job even before the business cards are printed.

"Let Baer do the suck-up stories," I tell her. "Trust me, you won't be happy if you let the suits guide your future."

"I'd have a future, at least."

It does make me sad. When I first signed on for journalism, the bar was pretty low and the cotton was high. All the ad guys had to do was go to the two big downtown department stores once a week and come back with a wheelbarrow full of money. Now people like Sarah, more talented and much more driven than I was at her age, have to make deals with the devil all the time. We keep losing good young ones to "media relations" jobs, where they get paid to hide the truth from their former compatriots.

"And I guess this is all connected with me trying to find that girl, the one Chenault was banging," Sarah says.

I have to admit that it all seems to be coming together.

"And the Tweety Bird killings . . ."

I am silent.

"Shit," she says. I think I might have reeled her in, at least temporarily, from the dark side.

MY MEETING WITH Thomas Jefferson Blandford V is at three. Andi doesn't know about this and, I hope, won't. I do have to get a couple of things straight with young Quip, though.

We meet at a place on Main Street that has a bar upstairs and around back. I prefer it because it's one of the few places in town where I can drink alfresco without inhaling bus fumes.

Quip's there when I arrive, nursing some kind of beer in a multicolored bottle that indicates it might taste like honey and cranberries. I order a Miller.

"So," I say to young Master Blandford after we've dispensed with scant pleasantries, "I understand you've been threatening my daughter."

He seems surprised by the direct approach. In the Blandfords' world, they use stilettos instead of meat cleavers.

"No. No. I don't know what you mean. We talked, but . . ."

I pull my chair a little nearer to the table separating us, close enough that my gut is pushing against it.

"I heard that you made some kind of reference to the baby having a 'white trash' upbringing," I continue, speaking softly, making serious eye contact. "The thing is, Quip, he'd be growing up pretty much the way I did, and I think I turned out all right. That's just my opinion, but do you think I'm white trash? If you think so, we can move on up to the next step."

Quip is looking around, maybe for a witness.

"Look," he says, holding his palms out, "I was pissed off. I didn't mean it. I really want to marry her."

"Well, I guess that'll have to be her decision, won't it?"

He clears his throat.

"But he'll be my son, too."

I assure Quip that Andi will want him to be a part of her son's life.

"The thing is, though, she isn't interested in marrying you. She thinks, to put it bluntly, that you're a bit of a fuckup. After checking with some people, I kind of have to agree with her."

It's amazing what doesn't get prosecuted if your daddy has enough money. I recount the two DUI arrests I know about that didn't make it onto Master Quip's permanent record, reduced to speeding and reckless driving. As someone whose drinking and driving issues don't get swept away, I particularly take offense at this abuse of power. Peachy Love is a wonderful source.

And then, there was the cocaine bust. Thomas Jefferson Blandford IV must have paid a king's ransom to get that one knocked down to probation and keep his son out of jail. The amount of coke in Quip's car usually would have earned a trip to a medium-security federal prison for a few years, maybe ten to twenty if he were of the wrong ethnic persuasion.

I am appalled that my daughter has been living with such, to use Quip's word, trash.

"How do you know all that?"

I explain that I am, after all, a reporter. I also explain that I am sure we can come to an agreement here: I don't write a story about the inequality of our justice system with the Blandfords as Exhibit A, and he stops leaning on my pregnant daughter.

"Plus, I won't have to kill you," I add, smiling to let him know I'm only kidding.

"Besides," I tell him as we part, "you can't be calling us 'white trash.' The baby will be one-eighth African American. I think your great-great-grandaddy would have called him an octoroon."

I leave him pondering that.

I ARRIVE AT Cindy's condo just after six. When she shows me in, allowing me only a chaste peck on the cheek, Mary Kate Kusack Brown is already there. She's sitting on the living-room couch, nervous as a cat.

She looks a little like Ronnie, but not too much, for which she must be grateful.

We chat for a minute or two, but she wants to cut to the chase.

"He was at my place," she says. "I told the police that. I don't think they believed me."

I mention the images they got from his computer. She seems a little shocked, and I'm wondering if she'll be asking her brother to do any more babysitting, just to be on the safe side.

She frowns and then shrugs.

"Ronnie hasn't always been the best at looking out for himself. He's done some kind of crazy things."

She confirms that her brother was at her house at eight or so the night of the eleventh, and that he was there until sometime after eleven.

"He said he spoke to your neighbors, but they didn't see him."

"That's right. I imagine they could identify his voice."

"But there's nothing you know of that would keep you from backing up his story?"

Again, a little hesitation. She looks away.

"No. Nothing. Ronnie's been good. He's always trying to look out for me and the kids. And Cord, too."

"Cord?"

"His—rather, our—brother."

She goes on to explain that their older brother, living up in Ohio, sends her money sometimes.

I note that it's nice to have family watching your back. I'm not quite sure how she takes it.

CHAPTER FOURTEEN

Monday

The first thing I see when I fetch the morning paper from the other side of my front door is the story on Wat Chenault and the slave graveyard. It's on the local front instead of A1, maybe because Wheelie sees this as mitigating circumstances when Chenault hauls the paper into court. The story is careful to give full credit to the *Scimitar*, so everyone knows it's not our fault. We didn't want to report the news, but they made us do it. I guess they're going to have to wait a couple of days to run Baer's puff piece on what a gift to humanity the fat man is.

Goat Johnson is in town, and we're planning to meet over at Joe's Inn and tell lies. Custalow is off this morning, so he's coming along, too. Andy Peroni and R.P. McGonnigal are going to meet us there. Old home week.

Abe sees the note stuck on my car's windshield before I do. It's pretty much along the same lines as the first one, only a bit more threatening.

"You and the cops are idiots," it starts out. "If you don't turn Ronnie Sax loose by Thursday, I start hunting again. I'm hungry for more Tweety Birds. Maybe that little bitch daughter of yours is next."

I recognize the handwriting. Same as before. This asshole has definitely upped the stakes.

Custalow looks at it.

"Don't you need to show that to the cops?"

Yes, I do.

THE CHAT WITH Ronnie Sax's sister was somewhat enlightening. The other brother, she told me, had been kind of in and out of their lives. I gather he's been, even by Ronnie's standards, a little troubled. The night of the eleventh, Ronnie seems to be accounted for, unless he managed to murder Jessica Caldwell before he arrived at eight and then deposited her body in the train station while he was also spending the evening with his sister and nieces. And Mary Kate was sure the neighbors would vouch for hearing Ronnie's voice at some point in the evening, she thinks between nine thirty and ten. Now, though, we have yet another mash note from somebody out there who isn't Ronnie Sax. And now it's gotten personal. I need to talk to Andi.

I CALL THE chief's office and, after I tell his secretary—excuse me, administrative aide—what I've got, L.D. Jones calls me back in five minutes.

I ask him if he would like to see the note.

I heard him sigh.

"Yeah, dammit, I would. Can you bring it by?"

I resist the urge to make him say "please." It's such a pleasure to have L.D. in my debt. It must be killing him. He's got the guy who did it in jail, except now maybe he doesn't.

I make a copy of the note and take it to the chief before we meet Goat, R.P. McGonnigal and Peroni. L.D. doesn't seem very grateful. He does have the grace to ask me if my daughter needs some police protection. I tell him, no, what she needs is to quit her damned bartending job and lie low until we settle this monster's hash.

I tell him that I'm not reporting on the latest note yet, although conditions might change. He seems to know that's the best deal he's going to get.

"DO YOU THINK he's going to let that Sax guy go?" Custalow asks me back in the car.

"Not a chance. He's going to need more than this."

L.D. did seem a little worried, though, when he got to the part about the guy threatening to go hunting again. I haven't mentioned yet my suspicions about Wat Chenault. No sense in worrying our overburdened chief unduly.

I call Andi and tell her I need to see her. She can work me in before her shift starts at four.

FRANCES XAVIER "GOAT" Johnson is his usual bullshitting self. They were able to commandeer the big table at the back of Joe's and are in full force when we get there.

"Do you remember the Church Hill tunnel?" Peroni asks me while we're sitting down. It has obviously been the topic of spirited conversation. "Goat says we spent the night there. He's full of crap, right?"

I tell him yeah, of course I remember the tunnel.

When we were teenagers, somebody told us about the locomotive that got buried underneath Church Hill, all those men buried alive and their bodies never recovered. Since the corpse of the Tweety Bird Killer's third victim turned up there at the entrance, a new generation has become familiar with the story, with poor Lorrie Estrada added to the tunnel's lore and legend.

The entrance was still there in 1977, so we felt duty bound, being badass Oregon Hill boys, to go explore it.

Goat had a car, and we finally found the entrance, almost covered over by weeds. I remember it was damp and spooky. We went what seemed like a long way, but it was probably just a few hundred yards, before we were blocked. We were going to spend the night there, but it was just too damn weird, even for us. Goat, of course, remembers us staying all night and seeing some weird light at the end. Goat's imagination sometimes gets the better of him.

"Well," he says, "the way I remember it, we didn't go home until dawn."

I mention the body that was dumped there in March.

"I hope they fry that motherfucker," R.P. says.

I tell him I hope so, too, and that I hope they have the right motherfucker.

"What I've heard about this guy," he says, "I'd say just pull the switch and let God sort it all out."

We give Goat shit about high-hatting us. He is actually wearing a suit. I guess it comes with the job. He's president of some half-ass college in Ohio, and there are three or four alums in town who might die and leave their alma mater some money if Goat kisses their asses with enough gusto.

He's still Goat, though, after three beers.

"To tell you the truth," he says, lowering his voice like we're wired for sound, "it's hard to have much respect for an institution of higher learning that would have me as its president."

We quickly agree. They order another round, but I have to go and meet Andi. Talking about the tunnel has me thinking, though. R.P. says he'll give Custalow a ride back to the Prestwould.

Andy Peroni asks me if I've gotten back in his sister's good graces yet. I tell him I'm still trying and ask him to put in a good word for me.

"You mean lie to my baby sister?"

Yeah, I tell him, if that's what it takes.

MY DAUGHTER ISN'T too happy when I tell her what the latest note said. She's even less happy when I tell her she has to quit her job for a little while.

"I'm not letting that son of a bitch rule my life," she says.

I point out that he's already permanently curtailed four young women's lives.

"But they weren't careful," she says. "They didn't know what they were doing. Besides, I can't quit. I need the money."

I assure her that, between her mother and stepfather and me, we can take care of her until we get to the bottom of this. I also assure her that this isn't going to take long. I'm not so positive about that, but I like to paint a cheery picture.

"If that bastard comes around here," Peggy says, "he's gonna get some of this."

She pulls a pistol from the silverware drawer and waves it around a little. Great, my dope-delirious mother is also now armed.

"Where did you get that thing?"

"It belonged to Les," she says as I turn the barrel away from Andi and me. "He said I might need it someday."

I ask her if she knows how to shoot it.

"I had a pistol all the time you were growing up. Just got rid of it a few years ago."

I am amazed. I ask her why I never knew this.

"I never had to use it," she says. "With a couple of my boyfriends and my second husband, I was tempted, but I resisted the urge."

She laughs, and I realize it's the first time I've heard my mother laugh since Les died. A small thing, but it does seem like a step toward the sunlight.

I tell Andi I'll go by Havana 59 and tell them the news.

"No, you won't," she says. "What do you think I am, ten years old?"

She pauses and sighs.

"I'll tell them myself."

I FINALLY FIND the tunnel entrance. It looks even more overgrown than it was all those years ago. It looks completely impenetrable now. I manage to get filthy walking and crawling through the mud. They still have the crime scene tape up, and it doesn't look like anybody's been back in the last six months. I can't even figure how somebody got a body up here. Maybe he made her walk up and then raped and killed her.

By the time I get back down to where my car is, it's starting to get dark. The wind or something is making a whistling noise, coming out of the mouth of the cave. I am pretty sure Goat Johnson is wrong about us spending the night here. I don't think we had balls enough.

ONE GOOD THING to come out of last night's meeting with Sax's sister is that I do have another date with the lovely Cindi Peroni tonight.

When I get back, though, intent on taking a quick shower and making myself as presentable as is possible for a fifty-three-year-old bald man who needs to lose weight, my plans get hijacked. Literally.

As I lock the car, I feel something hard push into my back.

"Get in," a voice says. It doesn't sound like a request.

I'm pushed into the backseat of a van I didn't notice before. The doors lock. Seated beside me, taking up way too much space, is the guy who obviously orchestrated this meeting.

The one with either a very hard finger or a gun gets in, too, and I'm wedged in the middle. Another guy, the driver, takes off.

"I understand," Wat Chenault says, "you've been asking some people about me."

I try to talk my way out of it, explaining that we're just doing a story on Top of the Bottom because our rival, the mighty *Scimitar*, beat us to it and now we have to catch up.

Chenault interrupts me midbullshit.

"Shut up," he says. "I'm not talking about the damn colored graves, although I'd surely like to know how that ghetto rag got it. Maybe you people have your own old boy system."

He smirks at me. I promise myself I will hit him when I can do it without getting shot.

"No, I'll let my lawyer handle all that. Just more proof of how you all are out to get me. What I want to talk about is that Adkins girl."

I'm not stunned. Maybe Johnny Grimes tipped him off. Maybe Sarah gave somebody too much information while she was searching. Whatever, there isn't much use in denying that I'm trying to find a girl who went missing more than a decade ago, after she helped ruin Wat Chenault's political career.

I ask him what he wants.

"What I want is for you to leave me the fuck alone. I haven't seen that little bitch since all that mess happened, and I don't need you stirring up shit that's long since been of no interest to anyone but your nosy ass."

I ask him if he's been writing any anonymous notes lately. I'm hoping that'll get a rise out of him, even though it might also get my butt kicked, or worse. I'm pretty sure I can make enough noise and cause enough havoc here on Broad Street to keep Chenault and his goons from doing me serious bodily harm.

He surprises me, though, by looking genuinely surprised.

"What the fuck would I do that for?" he asks. I let the subject drop.

Chenault shakes his head.

"You're a weird son of a bitch," he says. "I can't believe somebody hasn't put you out of your misery yet."

We're almost beyond the city limits, and I'm getting ready to do something drastic when Chenault tells the driver to turn around. The guy does an illegal U-turn. Five minutes later, we're back at the Prestwould parking lot.

We sit there for half a minute, me jammed between the other thug and Chenault.

"You can go to the police with this," the fat man says, "but we'll all swear that you got in on your own accord, and that we just had a nice, friendly chat about why you're messing around in my business."

He motions for the guy on my left to get out. I start to follow him. Chenault puts his meaty paw on my shoulder.

"Last warning," he says. "I'm not going to let my life get ruined by some pissant reporter."

I get out. Chenault rolls his window down when I walk to the other side, headed for the front door.

"You better be nice to me," he says. "After my lawyer gets through with you all, I might be your new boss."

He seems to find this amusing. I opt, for once, to shut up.

BACK INSIDE, I realize I was supposed to pick up Cindy five minutes ago.

I call, explaining that I've gotten a little tied up, and that I'll be over in thirty minutes. Actually, it'll be a good hour, by the time I shower and change.

"I don't know, Willie," Cindy says. "Maybe we ought to just make it another time. I've got a paper to do anyhow."

I observe that it's been some time since one of my dates begged off because of homework. Cindy's about a semester from getting the degree that marriage and kids delayed.

I don't push it, though. Truth be told, I'm a little freaked out by my most recent close encounter with the fat man. I maybe need some time to digest all this.

Cindy promises that my rain check will be honored.

CHAPTER FIFTEEN

Tuesday

Sarah still doesn't have any good news for me on the Leigh Adkins front.

"I thought I'd found her," she tells me when I stop in the office after breakfast. "There was this woman, same name, same age, up near Winchester. But when I called her, 'she' turned out to be a 'he.' Who the hell names their boy Leigh, anyhow?"

I conjecture that maybe his parents were hoping for a girl.

Sarah has used every source she can find, computer and otherwise, some in Virginia and some throughout the country. Nothing. She suggests that maybe I ought to hire a private detective. I tell her I don't think Wheelie would sign off on that as a business expense, although he probably should.

"Leigh Adkins has probably gotten married and has her husband's name now," Sarah says, "although she didn't show up on any marriage licenses, at least in this part of the world. When I marry, I'm going to keep my name, at least on my bylines."

I tell her I think she's right. There's no sense in wasting all those years she's spent building an identity. She looks to see if I'm jerking her chain. I assume a straight face and thank her for all her efforts. I also tell her about the second letter.

"Damn, Willie. When are you going to write something about this?"

I tell her that she's doing the Wat Chenault beat for now.

"I'm not so sure anybody's going to be doing it after the story this morning."

"New publisher on the warpath?"

"That is so politically incorrect. You probably want the Redskins to keep their name, too."

I tell her it doesn't really matter much to me, and it matters less to Custalow, who actually has a horse in this race, being of the Pamunkey tribe. He just wants them to stop sucking on Sunday afternoons.

But, yes, Ms. Dominick is not happy today. She had to approve us rewriting the story that the *Scimitar*, with a little help from their friend, ran on Sunday. But she's already been on the phone with Chenault's lawyer. I learned that from Sandy McCool, who gets paid less and does more work than anyone else on the fourth floor since they got rid of half the administrative assistants/secretaries up there. I haven't noticed any shortage of executives yet. Some of the poor bastards probably have had to learn to make their own coffee.

I promise Sarah that we're soon going to write something about this whole mess. Patience, I remind her, is a virtue.

"Getting our asses beat by the *Scimitar* isn't," she reminds me.

I assure her that the *Scimitar* won't be scooping us anymore.

"Not unless somebody feeds them another story," she says as she walks away.

Wheelie catches me before I can escape. I'm supposed to take Peggy out for a visit with Philomena sometime before I come to work for real. I ask Wheelie if it can wait. He assures me it can't.

He leads me up to the fourth floor. Sandy McCool offers a perfunctory nod and asks me how I'm doing, as if I didn't just call her a couple of hours ago. Sandy gives nothing away, which is why she's still here. People with brains—and some of the suits do have brains—know Sandy has information that she would never divulge, unless someone did something to piss her off, like, say, firing her.

Rita Dominick has put her stamp on the late James Grubbs's office. All Grubby's diplomas and Chamber of Commerce and Better Business Bureau awards, along with the one Virginia Press Association plaque he scored back when he was an honest journalist, are gone. In their stead are the sundry advertising plaudits our new boss has snagged over the years, along with three diplomas and pictures of her kids, and husband, who looks a little beaten-down. Two of the diplomas are the kind of graduate degrees you get by taking courses at night and on weekends in lieu of more rewarding hobbies like drinking and smoking. The third, her undergraduate one, causes me to do a double take. Did our new publisher really get her degree from one of those fly-by-night colleges you see advertised on TV, the ones that used to make their pitches on matchbook covers? I see her, out of the corner of my eye. She has a "you wanna make something of it?" look. No, I do not. I suck in a smirk and pretend that I think the University of Western New England is a laudable place (if, indeed it has a corporeal life) at which to improve one's mind.

"We're in a bind," Rita Dominick says by way of breaking the ice, which feels deep enough to drive an eighteen-wheeler over.

She tells us about her chat with Wat Chenault's lawyer. No newspaper these days can afford to pay to defend a lawsuit, let alone lose one. It's why we're so chickenshit, or at least now we have an excuse.

"We didn't have any choice," Wheelie begins. "The *Scimitar* . . ."

Dominick cuts him off. We all know she approved our rewrite of the story about Chenault's goons, and maybe Chenault himself, conspiring to conceal the fact that they unearthed human remains in the Bottom. She needs something else to pin on us, or at least one of us, if she's going to pass the buck down to the little folk.

"Chenault's lawyer says he has reason to believe that somebody from our paper gave that story to the *Scimitar*." When she says "somebody," she looks at me.

"The best I can gather," our publisher goes on, "the one person here who was most interested in our not dropping our investigation into Mr. Chenault was you."

I can lie with the best of them. I extol the journalistic capabilities of the *Scimitar*'s fine staff. Given truth serum, I would opine that most of them couldn't find their asses with both hands.

And, speaking of truth serum, Ms. Dominick then turns the burner on this conversation up a notch.

"Do you swear that you didn't leak that story to the *Scimitar*'s staff?"

I swear that I did not. (Hell, I didn't leak it to the staff. I told Earl Pemberton-Wise, and he told his reporter to interview me about it.)

"Are you willing to take a lie detector test?"

It's time for a little moral indignation. I can do that, even when I'm in the wrong. It's a gift.

"Hell, no," I tell her. "I won't take a lie detector test for you or anybody else. If you don't trust me, you ought to just fire my ass right now. Damn! I can't believe this."

I look toward Wheelie, who looks a little pale, then get up and start to leave. I'm bluffing with a pair of threes right now, but I'm not a bad poker player.

"Wait," our publisher says. "Come back here. I don't mean to impugn your honesty. But if somebody did leak that story, his head is going to roll. And I will find out, eventually."

Maybe she will and maybe she won't. It does seem, though, that I'd better come up with some goods on the upstanding Mr. Chenault very soon. At least, city officials are now crawling out of bed with Top of the Bottom, which the mayor has been wholeheartedly approving up to this point. In a city where half the population is African American, some of whose ancestors might be moldering beneath Wat Chenault's little scheme, it is time to tread lightly. All construction on the project is halted until, as the mayor so elegantly put it, "we can get to the bottom of this."

I can see why Chenault would like to take a pound or two of flesh off us. He hasn't even bothered to file papers against the *Scimitar*, I'm sure. Other than office supplies, I doubt there's much for him to squeeze out of that noble news organ.

Wheelie and I leave. We're on the elevator when my managing editor, not usually given to the theatrical gesture, stops the car between floors.

"I know who leaked that story," he tells me. "I have a few contacts, too, you know. Did you really think that wouldn't get out?"

It's no use pretending. Wheelie knows, and if he wanted me fired, he'd have settled my hash back in the publisher's office.

I wait for it.

"Just be sure," he tells me, actually putting his finger in my face, "that you nail the son of a bitch. Whatever you're sniffing after, you better nail him so good that his lawyers can't touch us."

"Does that mean I'm back on the Wat Chenault beat?"

"Not officially. I think Chenault suspects you're somehow behind this. You'll pass whatever you know on to Sarah Goodnight. It'll be her byline on it."

Well, that's something. And I appreciate Wheelie putting the news ahead of his butt for a change. I once suggested, in an ill-advised burst of frustration, that he grow a pair.

Maybe he has. With the paper in imminent danger of being sold to the Friedman chain or one of its soulless contemporaries, maybe Wheelie's feeling he doesn't have much to lose. If we're looking at a scenario where our already diminished staff is cut in half to make the stockholders happy, then we might as well make some good journalism before the ax falls.

I PICK UP Peggy, who seems almost straight today, and we head out to Philomena's. I've been promising to take her to visit my late father's cousin. Andi asks to come along.

I ask Peggy, on the way over, how she's doing.

"Hanging in there," is her tepid response. Andi reaches up from the backseat and rubs her shoulder.

It does seem to lift her spirits to be with Philomena, though. It warms my jaded heart to see the two of them embrace. Peggy and I didn't have a whole lot of family when I was growing up on the Hill. Most of her kin more or less disowned her for having a child with a black man. And his family wasn't a factor, since she never married Artie Lee, who wrapped his car around a very large tree before I was out of diapers.

Andi seems to fit right in, though, fascinated still to discover family she never knew she had until recently.

Richard comes home for lunch. He's working as a mechanic, at a shop four blocks away. There was some kind of automotive mechanic program at one of the prisons where he spent most of his adult life, and he took advantage of it, in the unlikely event that he someday might need to find a job.

"That was good, what you did for Momma and Miss Sophia," he says.

I tell him that I didn't do much. It was the *Scimitar* that forced us to write about it.

He gives me a look that tells me he maybe knows more about that episode than my publisher does. News travels fast, often without the aid of trained professional journalists. "I Heard It Through the Grapevine" somehow pops into my head.

"However it happened," Richard says, "we appreciate it."

He asks me if my car needs a tune-up. Probably, I tell him. All I know about cars is to change the oil every six thousand miles or so, empty the ashtray every now and then, and get it inspected once a year.

He tells me to bring it by and he'll let me know what needs fixing.

"Might even be able to do it myself," he says.

I promise him I will bring back my old Honda. It would be rude to do otherwise.

Peggy's in such fine spirits that, when it's time for me to go to work, Philomena says she'll drive her and Andi home when they're through visiting. I suppose Awesome Dude will have to dine alone tonight.

Thinking about the Dude makes my pinball brain bounce onto something else, something my peripatetic friend told me about the night Kelli Jonas was murdered. I can't quite get my mind around what's bothering me about it. It's like an itch in that little spot in the middle of your back that you can't quite reach.

IT'S A QUIET night back at the paper. I have time to do a little digging. Sarah's writing something tomorrow about Top of the Bottom being halted, but I'm giving L.D. Jones a much-undeserved break and not writing about the letter left on my windshield yesterday. On the off chance that the cops can make something out of this, I'll give our boys in blue a couple of days.

I don't want to give Johnny Grimes another call, since there's a pretty good chance he told Chenault about the last one. There are a couple of things I'd like to know, though, while Sarah tries to find Leigh Adkins.

R.P. McGonnigal has a friend—steady boyfriend, actually—who is a private detective. I don't intend to put him on the trail of Wat Chenault's long-ago underage sex toy. There is something else, though, that I have in mind.

I've met the guy a couple of times. I think that he and R.P. might get married, if that ever becomes a possibility in our benighted commonwealth. We've joked about it, about the sheer goofiness of Abe, Andy, Goat and me standing there in tuxes while our old friend marries another man. For four Oregon Hill rednecks, we're pretty progressive, at least where our friends are concerned.

"If it makes R.P. happy," Custalow said, "it makes me happy."

The detective's name is, I swear, Sam Spadewell. Well, actually, I think his real first name is Robert or Ronald or something like that, but if you're a PI and your last name's Spadewell, how can you resist?

Sam is amenable to what I'm proposing. When we get around to talking about money, he says don't worry about it, that we'll work something out later.

He tells me a story.

"When I was like twenty-five or so, a friend and me, we got caught on a morals charge. You know, like doing it in the park. The cops loved to catch you, back then.

"We weren't hurting anybody. Nobody saw us except this nosy-ass cop that spent all his shift just trying to bust us."

It wouldn't have risen above a brief on B5, but this one state senator from Southside decided to go on a crusade against gays "defiling our public parks."

He made such a fuss about it that the city wound up prosecuting Sam and his friend.

"We got six friggin' months in jail," he says. "And I don't have to tell you who the fat fuck in the legislature was. I've been waiting."

Sometimes, I'm thinking, your turkeys do come home to roost.

CHAPTER SIXTEEN

Wednesday

I go over to the jail with Kate and Marcus. They're up to date on the second note now.

Ronnie Sax is informed that somebody has sent a second letter in an effort to get him out of jail.

"Well, whoever it is, I appreciate it," he says. He doesn't seem nearly as surprised at having a benefactor as I think he should be. That wheezy laugh of his is just a cough now. I don't think incarceration is agreeing with Ronnie.

"Who could've sent this?" Marcus asks.

Sax shrugs.

"Hell if I know. It might be good to start with the fucker who killed those girls, but I guess the cops are too damned lazy to get off theirs butts and find out. Or maybe you could."

Kate reminds him that we're about the only people on the planet right now who actually are trying to spring him. The replies we've gotten online about the case are along the lines of "Fuck him. Kill him now." I mention to him that he is not exactly the people's choice at the present time.

"Yeah," he says. "One of the cops showed me what they were writing about me. Damn, these people don't even know me."

I'm thinking that the fewer people really get to know Ronnie Sax, the better off he is.

Still we don't kill people just because they deserve it on general principles. If they did that, the newsroom would be even thinner than it is now. You've got to actually do the deed. As much as I dislike Ronnie Sax, I am not 100 percent sure he did the deed.

WHOEVER WANTS SAX sprung isn't kidding around.

The mail carrier comes just before I leave for work. One of the cool things about the Prestwould is the mail. They drop it through a slot in the front door of my unit, like something out of a 1930s movie, which makes sense, seeing as how the place was built in 1929. My bounty consists of the cable bill, the electricity bill, and a small envelope without a return address.

"Dear Asshole," the note begins, so I'm already pretty sure it isn't an invitation from some broker wanting to treat me to dinner in exchange for access to my vast savings, of which there aren't any. "Are you stupid? What part of 'you've got the wrong guy' don't you understand? Do I really have to send another Tweety Bird to the morgue to convince you? I'm getting a little hungry anyhow. How's that lovely daughter of yours, by the way? She's got a nice ass."

I resist the urge to crumple it up and throw it away. I'm still standing at the front door, so I punch it instead. It's solid metal, so that makes me feel much better.

I call Peggy's and speak with Andi. I emphasize, without reading her the note, that she should definitely not leave the house unchaperoned.

"You're starting to scare me," she says, and I tell her that that is my intention.

Andi tells me that the inestimable Quip Blandford called last night, all remorse and good intentions. He says he wants to at least "be friends," which is not a lot to offer, I guess, to the mother of your child. But I'm being unkind. Quip is apparently willing to do what we used to call the honorable thing, back when things were honorable.

I ask, with trepidation, how things stand now between her and her baby daddy. She worries me when she says that she isn't sure, but I understand. Maybe life with Thomas Jefferson Blandford V wouldn't be heaven on earth, but I doubt if Andi would ever have to tend bar or wait tables again.

I hang up and call L.D. Jones to tell him the third time is a charm. Now we have to go with the story. I can write this one, since it doesn't have anything—at least, not for now—to do with Wat Chenault.

"You can't do that," he says. "It's going to bust this thing wide open."

I remind him that I've given him a head start, but I don't see anybody behind bars yet.

He sighs and asks me to read this one to him. When I finish, he says, "Jesus Christ. Do you want us to have somebody keep an eye on your mom's place?"

I tell him that maybe that would be a good idea. Maybe L.D. Jones has a heart after all. But I wonder if I shouldn't just move Peggy, Andi and, yes, Awesome Dude in with Custalow and me. I hope Peggy knows how to use that damn pistol.

Then, I call Marcus and let him and Kate know about Letter Number Three.

"They've got to release that son of a bitch now," Marcus says. I'm not so sure they have to do anything, but the heat's on, for sure.

IN THE NEWSROOM, it's business as usual.

Baer's puff piece on Chenault is running tomorrow. Meanwhile, Sarah is working the traps still, looking for Leigh Adkins. And she's been doing some digging on her own, so to speak. She's found another worker down in the Bottom who'll back up the story I planted in the *Scimitar*.

"I think Wheelie's going to let us run it," she says. I'm starting to think that Wheelie really is becoming testicularly enhanced. No way he's run this one past our new publisher first. With all the rumors of our impending sale, I guess we're all kind of getting into what Enos Jackson calls NTL mode. Nothing To Lose.

"We're going to run good Wat, bad Wat, the same day?"

"I don't know, but that Baer piece has been ready for two days. Maybe Wheelie figures one will balance out the other.

I, for one, don't think there is a good Wat Chenault, but maybe this will lop a few hundred thousand off the damages.

Wheelie's in his office. I walk in and shut the door. I've never seen Wheelie drink hard liquor, but he has this red Solo cup in his hand, and I'm pretty sure the clear stuff inside isn't water.

I bring him up to date about the letters. Wheelie isn't drunk, but he's a little looser than usual. I'm thinking he should imbibe more often.

"You got three of them?" he says. I explain, before he can ask, that I've been holding out to give the cops a chance to nab whomever it is.

"Now, though, it's time to write something."

"Are you going to mention your daughter?"

I've thought about that.

"No, I'm just going to say that he has made threats against a specific individual, who is getting police protection."

"It's gonna make the cops look kind of silly."

I tell him that isn't my intention, but I've given them all the leeway an honest journalist can afford to give a police department. Time to get out the ink and newsprint and let the populace know why they usually have the trial before the hanging.

As I leave to write my story, I feel obliged to ask him if he's really going to run another Wat Chenault story tomorrow.

"Bet your ass," he says. "We're going to get sued, we might as well go for the big bucks."

Wheelie's laugh isn't as grating as Ronnie Sax's. It's actually kind of pleasant. It is the laugh of someone who has crossed that line beyond which you're going to do what ought to be done, and you don't really give a shit what happens next.

It is a line with which I am familiar. I perhaps should tell Wheelie that virtue, while it feels as good as a shot of quality vodka, can give you an awful hangover.

"You really ought to let your editors know, once in a while, what the hell you're doing," Wheelie says as I shut the door. He's right, but sometimes it just muddies things up if everybody knows everything. I'm more of a need-to-know kind of guy.

So tomorrow's paper might be worth seventy-five cents after all.

We're going to have a story on A1 that says a certain reporter has gotten three notes in the last week from an unincarcerated individual who claims that he, not Ronnie Sax, is the Tweety Bird Killer.

We're going to have another story on A1, a fluffy, feel-good feature by Mark Baer on Wat Chenault.

And the icing on top, we're going to run Sarah's story on B1 offering more evidence that the minions of the upstanding Mr. Chenault have been covering up, literally, the remains of long-dead slaves because they're getting in the way of his real-estate scheme.

People with enough attention span to remember Baer's puff piece while they're reading Sarah's story might think there's some kind of disconnect here.

Me, I'm just trying to connect all the dots.

CHAPTER SEVENTEEN

Thursday

Sally Velez phones, waking me up to tell me that Ronnie Sax is now, at least for the time being, a free man.

She got a call from someone she knows down at police headquarters. I wonder if it's Peachy Love and feel a twinge of jealousy. Is Peachy cheating on me, spreading some of that good information to somebody else? I doubt it. Peachy's pretty careful. She knows being the source for even one journalist is tricky enough. She's not the promiscuous type.

"He's already out?"

"That's what I hear. Somebody came and picked him up this morning. I think his lawyer posted bail."

Thanks, Marcus, for telling me. And thanks to you, too, Kate, my landlord and ex-wife. Oh, well. I neglected to tell them that the story about the letters was running today. Tit for tat.

The piece I did for this morning's paper was, against my will, posted at eleven last night, a truly dumbass move. One of the TV stations was, for once, alert enough to check our website and get it in at the tail end of their late news. And, of course, there are the Internet insomniacs who can't wait until the next morning to read our paper set on newsprint. Maybe Marcus Green was one of them, although I can't quite envision that. We do make the online freeloaders pay a pittance now for the privilege, but if you had to staff a newsroom on what it costs to breach our tissue-paper firewall, you'd be down to about six reporters and editors. It is unlikely I would be one of them.

It did light a fire under some people, though. There were more than 200 responses online. Their reactions were, as usual, reasoned and considerate of others. If only. Most of our online readers seem sure about everything and equally sure that anyone who disagrees with them is an idiot.

Thus there were the ones who are positive that those letters from outside Ronnie Sax's cell were proof not only that he is innocent but that the entire police department should be rounded up and shot for (a) arresting and scarring for life the wrong man and (b) letting a deranged killer continue to wander our streets.

And there were the ones who, having had a good look at Ronnie Sax and a passing knowledge of his relationship with girls and young women, want to see him executed just because they've decided they don't like the son of a bitch. They also want those who disagree to eat shit and die.

I call Marcus. He posted bail for Sax, who is still on the hook for charges related to pornography. Marcus, who makes no apologies for not giving me a heads-up, says he thinks anything Sax might have done is going to amount to nothing more than a very light sentence and a good talking-to, seeing as how he has innocently languished in jail lo these many days and soon will be suing the pants off the police department.

"So," Marcus says, "the cops have still got a psychopath out there. I'd hate to be L.D. Jones right now."

He's right. I've got my ideas about who ought to be replacing Ronnie Sax down at the lockup, but the whole thing is so crazy that I don't even want to broach the subject with the chief just yet. I mean, who the hell is going to believe that Wat Chenault is a deranged psychopath? He might have had an itch for young girls once upon a time, but if he's ever been arrested for anything bigger than a speeding ticket, it's been expunged from his record. I know. I've looked.

My private detective is on the case, and Sarah Goodnight's still out there beating the bushes for Leigh Adkins. A guy who cares enough to take me for a little ride with his goons, and implies a longer, less pleasant ride is in the offing if I don't butt out of his business, just makes me want to butt harder.

THERE'S PLENTY TO write about today. First, though, I make a run by Ronnie Sax's apartment. There are two TV camera crews there already. Mr. Sax, it appears, has left the building. When I call Marcus, Kate answers the phone and says they don't know where he is, either, but she's sure he's around somewhere. After all, why would he jump bail? Since the bail was posted by Marcus, I'm sure at least one person in Richmond is hoping Sax is just hiding out from the news media and not making a dash for the border.

I recognize one of the women I spoke with earlier about Ronnie. She says nobody's seen him.

"Nobody wants to see him, either," she says. I don't see any welcome-home cards or flowers at the recently sprung Mr. Sax's digs. Instead, somebody painted "Leave, asshole" on the door.

Back at the office, I call L.D. Jones for a comment. His aide says he will hold a press conference at eleven.

THE CHIEF DOESN'T look happy. The mayor hasn't joined him for this one. The mayor only shows up for happy news. L.D. frowns when he sees me, although Peggy says a very conspicuous cop car has been cruising by the house on a regular basis, for which I am grateful. I feel for L.D., but it's become pretty obvious that somebody other than Ronnie Sax is on the prowl, and people need to know, whether it makes the cops look like assholes or not. L.D. prefers to make the arrest before the press conference, but this time it can't be that way.

He says Sax is still a "person of interest," but that the police are going "in new directions" and will have a suspect in custody "in the near future." He says this is based on new evidence that has recently come to light. Right. "Come to light" because you couldn't keep us in the dark any longer. Asked to be a little more specific about who the suspect might be and how far in the future we might have to wait for him to be apprehended, the chief says he can't talk anymore about any "ongoing investigation." I don't even bother raising my hand.

He does surprise me, though, by asking me to drop by after the grilling is over.

In his office, L.D. looks haggard.

"Three o-damn-clock," he says. "That's when I got the call from one of my lieutenants. Said they were hearing from everybody out there on the street. Been up since three o-damn-clock. Thanks to you."

I ask L.D. if he really wants to let some stone killer wander around loose out there.

"We were on the trail," he says, but I know he's bullshitting. When I ask him whose trail, he says he can't tell me. "Now we might scare the SOB off."

I note that a person who sends repeated notes telling you you've got the wrong man and threatening more mayhem isn't too likely to be scared off.

"That's what I wanted to ask you about," he says, stifling a yawn. "If you get anything else from this guy, you're going to tell us, aren't you?"

I run the numbers over in my mind, trying to come up with a decent compromise. L.D. wants me to tell him everything. I'm sure Wheelie wants me to tell the cops nothing. Somewhere between everything and nothing, there's got to be a number that will piss everybody off just a little.

"You can have a twenty-four-hour head start," I tell the chief. "If I get another note at ten in the morning, I won't put it online until ten the next morning."

The chief tries to get that up to thirty-six, and then thirty hours, but I'm firm with twenty-four.

"You ain't giving me much time," he says.

You already know somebody else is out there, I remind him. You're already beating down every door in town.

L.D. shakes his head.

"I was sure," he says. "I was sure we had the right one. This guy has guilt written all over his ass."

"You never know," is all I can think to say.

On the way out, he stops me.

"If you've got any hunches about this, you'll tell me, right?"

I assure him he'll be the first to know. He doesn't look like he believes me.

THE STORY PRETTY much writes itself. Sax had a comment, released through Marcus to us and every other news outlet, that he was glad justice had been done at last. I hope he's right.

Sarah comes by and says she's pretty much tapped out on the Leigh Adkins front. If Ms. Adkins is in the land of the living, her whereabouts is beyond our meager talents. If she's in some unmarked grave or scattered in pieces across the countryside, it's not showing up on our radar screens.

"I don't know, Willie," Sarah says. "It's like she just vanished. And Wheelie's got two other stories I have to get cracking on."

That's what happens these days. The staff gets cut, and you don't have the luxury of turning a reporter loose on a story until the damn thing is wrestled to the ground. We get a story in a chokehold and then we have to let it escape while we go chase something else.

I check my e-mail. There are seven messages from readers wanting to rip me a new one for helping to clear a mass murderer. Two of them are more than vaguely threatening. Nobody's e-mailing to compliment me on my good work. The voice mail is similarly bile-heavy.

Meanwhile Wheelie's up to his ass in alligators over the story Sarah did this morning that will further cripple Wat Chenault's chances of ever seeing Top of the Bottom come to fruition. Neither he nor his lawyers were in the least appeased by the nice little blowjob piece Baer wrote, Wheelie says.

"One of our readers called in and wanted to know whether we were for him or agin' him," Wheelie says, failing miserably at trying to sound Southern.

"Our publisher was not amused," he adds. The red Solo cup on his desk looks about half full of ice and something the color of water. "She wants to take it out on Sarah. I told her this just fell into Sarah's lap, and if she wanted to blame somebody, she could blame me."

This truly is a new Wheelie I'm seeing, whether fortified by Dutch courage or just the knowledge that all our days around here could be numbered, so WTF. Mallory Wheelwright is young enough and has enough connections in other towns that he might be able to tell Rita Dominick to go pound sand.

So far, he adds, she hasn't chosen to take him up on his offer of shouldering the blame, but the day is young.

I'VE GOTTEN CHUCK Apple to fill in for me for a couple of hours tonight. I've got a hot date.

Cindy is giving me another chance after our last little get-together was curtailed by circumstances beyond my control. If somebody tries to abduct me tonight, he'd better have a big gun or a lot of friends.

We meet at Lemaire. I owe her something a little more high-end than Spaghetti Albert at Joe's after standing her up three days ago. Plus, Lemaire is one of those places where you can actually have a conversation with the person on the other side of the table, something my fifty-something ears appreciate.

She's waiting in the lobby when I get there. It's only five blocks from the paper, so I walk down, avoiding the urge to smoke the Camel that's calling my name. There is an outside chance I'll get to kiss Ms. Peroni, who is a bigot when it comes to cigarette breath.

She looks lovely. Her brown hair hangs down over those adorable ears I'm yearning to kiss. She has the same bright, mischief-promising eyes, the same mouth whose default position is a smile, those same dimples that made me fall for her when she came back into my life—Andy Peroni's kid sister all grown up—more than a year ago. Did I mention that she has a nice ass, too?

She affords me a chaste lip-kiss, making me glad I passed on the Camel. I've been more or less good with the drinking of late. It's been awhile since I was unable to account for my whereabouts the night before. The smoking, though, that's a bitch. It is a little easier when I don't drink, as those particular vices have a tendency to do a tag team on me, sometimes joined by that third vice, the one that has cost me three marriages so far, two of which were pretty good when Little Willie was under control. Still, cigarettes are the hardest to kick. Awesome says he knows a guy, living alfresco down by the river when the weather affords it, who has kicked heroin but still can't stop smoking.

We chat about this and that, testing the water. Eventually, between the onion soup and the duck breast, we fall back into a semblance of the easy bond we had before one of my more spectacularly appalling drunken binges screwed it up.

We're seated at right angles from each other. When I reach down and squeeze her left hand, she squeezes back for a couple of seconds before retreating and gracing me with those extremely kissable dimples.

"So," she says as we tuck into our main courses, "Ronnie Sax is free."

I note that his sister must be doing the happy dance.

Cindy surprises me by frowning and not saying anything for a few seconds.

Like a good reporter, I wait for it.

"You would think so," Cindy says.

I wait some more. Finally she can't help it.

"OK. I called her this afternoon. You know, to congratulate her and all. And you know what she said?"

I shake my head.

"She said that she hoped she had done the right thing. I asked her what she was talking about, and she said that there was more to it than she had let on, but she couldn't tell me. But I thought she wanted to."

Cindy said that when she pressed Ronnie's sister for more enlightenment, she said she had to go, that she had a call on the other line. When Cindy tried to call her back, the phone went to voice mail.

"So I don't know."

Me either, I tell her. I do lay out the basics of my suspicions about Wat Chenault, though. I probably shouldn't tell anybody else, even Cindy, about this right now. Maybe I'm just trying to impress her. I swear her to secrecy.

"You think he could be the Tweety Bird Killer?" She lowers her voice and leans close enough to me that I can smell her perfume, which I can't identify but would like to make mandatory for all women.

"I don't know what I think. I'm just trying to make sure we've got it right."

I walk her to her car after we share a strawberry rhubarb cobbler. ("Share" meaning she took a bite to be polite.) We do exchange a real kiss then.

"Oh, Willie," she says. "Why do the men in my life have to be such fuck-ups?"

I offer the opinion that fuck-ups probably are in the majority, and that maybe she should just settle for one who makes her happy most of the time and is capable of change.

She looks up at me. Her eyes are shining a little more than usual.

"And are you capable of change?"

I tell her there's no telling what a good woman could make of me.

"And you think I'm a good woman?"

It's time for the heavy artillery. I get down on one knee, right there on Franklin Street. Diners inside can see me if they choose to look. I tell her that she's the finest woman I've known (no sense in holding back now), and that I do truly believe in the gospel of hope, which says all things are possible.

"Possible, if not probable," she says. She smiles. I think she's relieved that I didn't reach into my pocket for a ring while I was down there.

I ask her if she's doing anything tomorrow night. She says she isn't, then stops.

"Damn," she says. "I promised two of my girlfriends that we'd go to Lulu's tomorrow night and listen to some music. You know, girls' night out and all that crap."

She seems genuinely sorry that she's busy.

"But I don't think I have anything doing Saturday," she says, and I tell her she does now.

We have another kiss for the road. I'm tempted to ask her if she'd like to come to my place for a drink, which we both would know was code for some doubles push-ups. I stop short. Our relationship now is a feral cat on the edge of the yard, likely to scatter and run at the least provocation.

I'M ONLY HALF an hour late getting back to the paper. I apologize to Chuck Apple. I definitely owe him a pint.

Nothing's going on, murder-wise. My phone is blinking. The first message consists of Peggy calling to tell me a joke

Awesome told her. I don't believe most people's mothers tell them scatological jokes, but she's the only mother I've had, so I don't know for sure. I'm just glad she's capable of sharing a laugh.

The next two messages are from more dissatisfied customers calling me bad names and blaming me for the police letting Ronnie Sax loose.

I delete those halfway through. They were starting to get repetitious. One guy calls me an asshole four times in forty-five seconds. No synonyms, buddy?

The fourth call, though, gets my attention.

"Way to go, dumbass," the voice, which I don't recognize, says. "You really don't know which end is up, do you?"

I hear the guy laugh, then he goes on.

"Know what I think? I think it's Tweety Bird hunting season again."

And then he hangs up.

I'm at least smart enough not to erase it. We don't have caller ID on the newsroom phones. Some of our best stories come from anonymous tips, and how can you be anonymous if I have your phone number?

Numbers can be traced, though, if the caller's careless. I somehow don't think this guy's careless.

It's after nine when I phone L.D. Jones's private number, the one he gave me earlier today. He assures me he will have someone working on it within the hour.

"You going to write something for the paper about that?" Sally Velez asks as soon as I hang up. She's the only one within earshot of my conversation.

I explain my deal with the chief. I can tell Sally this. She understands, like Wheelie probably couldn't, that the truth sometimes has to age a little bit.

CHAPTER EIGHTEEN

Friday

The number, as I suspected, is untraceable. The guy, whoever he is, probably bought one of those cheap-ass phones you use and throw away.

Well, I'm pretty sure the voice I heard didn't belong to Ronnie Sax. I'm equally positive it wasn't Wat Chenault.

The city is back in full-scale panic mode. Most of the citizenry is sure an unknown psychopathic killer is out there, hiding in the tall weeds and waiting to strike again. The rest think the police, with the help of me and the paper, have turned the real killer loose.

Over coffee, I check my office phone from home and discover I have twenty-seven messages. Nothing would make me happier than to erase them all and save my ears. Like most easy things, though, that's not always the smartest strategy.

Once, in my impetuous youth, I zapped all my phone messages after a week's vacation. Three days later, one of our state legislators rather spectacularly flipped from the Democrats to the Republicans, who made him a better offer. He gave the story to one of the TV stations. After being asked by our managing editor how I managed to get my ass handed to me by the talking heads, I called the guy. I was sorely pissed. I thought I had built a warm, caring relationship, based on my willingness not to print half of what I knew about him in exchange for certain tidbits.

"Hoss, I called you four days ago," he said. "The message said you were on vacation, so I held off until you got back. Hell, man, you snooze, you lose."

So I try not to snooze.

Most of the calls on my answering machine are just more of the same—angry fathers wanting to know what kind of an asshole would have a hand in turning a killer loose. About twenty seconds is enough for most of those before hitting the delete button.

But, eight calls into my thankless task, I'm glad that I did the hard thing, even if the message I get isn't exactly what I was expecting to hear.

"Mr. Black?" the voice says. "I understand you've been trying to find me. I used to be Leigh Adkins."

She leaves a number. If she isn't there when I call, she says someone can go find her. She says to ask for Piety.

THE FARM ISN'T that far out of Richmond. It takes me way less than an hour to get there. Being a city boy who didn't get out much until he was eighteen, I'm still amazed at how damned fast you hit open country when you leave Richmond. You go from corner bars to kudzu in about ten minutes. The place I'm looking for is a dozen or so miles off the interstate, so close to the Blue Ridge that you can see the mountains in the distance on a clear day like this.

THE GIRL WHO answered when I called the number the former Leigh Adkins gave me sounded somewhat blissed out, sort of like Peggy most mornings.

"Piety? Oh, yeah. Piety. Yeah. Wow. Just a minute."

After five minutes, another voice, a male one sounding somewhat more connected to solid ground, came on the line.

"What do you want with Piety?"

I explained that she had left me her number and asked me to call. I gave him my name. He set the phone down without further comment. I could hear sounds through the abandoned receiver. I think I heard a rooster crow.

After another five minutes, I hear a tentative voice:

"Hello?"

I explained, again, that I was trying to reach Piety.

"This is she."

She confirmed to me that she was the former Leigh Adkins. I asked if I could talk with her.

"We are talking."

"No. In person."

She was quiet for a moment, then said, "OK, I guess, if I can get permission. But you have to promise me something."

What I had to promise was that I would not tell anyone where she was or anything else about her.

"I heard that maybe they thought I was dead. I'm not. At least, my body's not dead. But Leigh Adkins, she's, like, long gone."

I assured her that my sole desire was to determine that Leigh Adkins, or whomever Leigh Adkins has morphed into, was still among the living and had not met with foul play.

She laughed, a little harder than what the situation called for.

"Foul play," she said. "That's funny. Mr. Black, I've met with lots of foul play. It just didn't kill me."

I mention that, while it's none of my business, her mother seemed anxious about her whereabouts.

"Well, you're right, Mr. Black. It is none of your business. But, if you want to reassure yourself that I'm alive, come on out. But I expect you to keep your promise."

I assure her that whatever secrets she has, they're safe with me. She seems too trusting, considering that we haven't ever met. Maybe being out of what we call civilization for more than a decade does that to you.

THE COMMUNE HAS been there for some time, out in an area full of cattle farms, rich come-heres doing the ego winery thing, and the occasional rebel flag. We used to write about it once in a while, but now it's nothing exotic, just part of the scenery.

There's not much to tell you you're there. I go by the entrance, off a poorly maintained county road, twice before I find it, just a half-hidden big-ass mailbox with "Solace" hand-painted on it. The rut road runs through half-abandoned fields and well-tended gardens, the latter being worked by an assortment of skinny people reliving the sixties.

The main house, which looks like it predates the Civil War, is more than a mile off the road. It's flanked by several modular units more or less imitating actual houses.

When I get out, I am besieged by a menagerie of dogs. Like their presumptive owners, they seem harmless. Chickens and goats wander in the background.

A young woman wearing a straw hat and overalls walks toward me.

"Hi," she says. "I'm Piety."

She did get permission to talk with me, although we chat in the presence of a scowling man-boy whom I'd like to bitch-slap as soon as I have what I need.

We drink something that passes for tea, and she tells me the story of her life. The man-boy, not all bad, offers me a toke from a full-figured doobie. I decline.

Leigh Adkins was not, it soon becomes clear, very happy with her life in her small Southside town. She says she'd run with a rough crowd, and that her early experiences with intimacy included some unwanted attention from a couple of her mother's boyfriends.

"When I complained to her, she just said you've got to go along to get along. 'Go along to get along.' She said it just like that."

Piety gives a short laugh, dry as a martini.

"I ran away. I didn't ever want to go back there again."

Things got a little rough, though. She says she was "rescued" by the good folks from Solace, who apparently wandered the streets of Richmond back then looking for people who needed saving. Might still be doing it for all I know.

"I was born again," she says, then is quick to assure me that this doesn't have anything to do with religion.

"This is my family now. We are all here together. We are one."

A little girl comes wandering in, barefoot and smiling, wearing a dress made by an amateur.

"Come here, Sunshine."

The little girl comes running to her. She's maybe five. She jumps up on her mother's lap.

I never know if Sunshine is the little girl's name or just what Piety calls her. When the former Leigh Adkins shows me her old driver's license, I'm assured that I have found her, and that she has found whatever she was looking for.

"Do you remember Wat Chenault?" I ask her.

She frowns for a minute, then brightens.

"Oh, the fat guy in Richmond. The one that got in so much trouble over me. Is he what this is all about? He isn't trying to find me, is he?"

I tell her my suspicions. She gets a good laugh out of them.

"Oh, my goodness," she says. "You've got to be kidding. He was one of the good ones. He never hit me or anything."

The man-boy lets her walk with me out to my car, which is accumulating a fine patina of red Virginia clay.

"You know," she says, as I'm about to leave, "I wouldn't have done this five years ago. Let you know I was alive, I mean. I just wanted to disappear into the earth, be part of it, invisible."

She says she did make one quick trip back to her hometown, incognito, for her big sister's funeral.

"I wore a hat and sunglasses, and I stood across the road from where they buried her. I felt bad, but it wasn't my life anymore."

She turns and looks off across the field.

"Now, though, I don't know. Maybe one day I'll show my sorry excuse for a mother that she has a granddaughter."

I mention that her mom probably wouldn't live forever, adding some bullshit about forgiveness and regret.

"Oh, I know about forgiveness," she says, fixing me with her bright blue eyes. "I can do forgiveness. I just don't want to be part of all that. I just want to be clean."

She sighs.

"Maybe someday I'll reconnect," she says. Then she grabs my right wrist, hard. She jabs two of her fingers into the soft underside of it. I wince.

"It's just that I want to do it on my own terms. You understand?"

I nod, and she lets go.

On the way back to town, I call Sarah.

"You can call off the dogs," I tell her. "Leigh Adkins is alive and well."

"SO," SARAH SAYS when I get back to the office, "we're back to square one?"

I explain about Ms. Adkins, declining even to give Sarah her new name. After all the digging she's done, she's not too happy about that, but a promise is a promise.

We're back in business on the Tweety Bird front. I write a story that will be ready to go unless pigs fly and our redoubtable police department finds this guy before deadline tonight.

We have a story, one way or the other. Just the fact that there's still a killer on the loose is enough kindling to keep the fire going on a daily basis. But it will burn a little brighter if I can also report that this maniac is still bragging about what he's going to do next. That ought to goose gun and ammo sales around here, like we're not overarmed already. It's so bad now that I'm afraid to give somebody the finger when they cut me off in traffic. A guy got shot doing that last week.

I check with Andi to make sure she and my unborn grandson are sticking close to home. Peggy assures me that she will shoot anyone who comes near my daughter looking even vaguely dangerous. I plead my case for caution and make a mental note to announce myself loudly when I pay my next visit to my mother.

And Sarah has another story on Top of the Bottom. The African American community has gotten new life in its efforts to keep the bulldozers at bay, thanks to the *Scimitar*'s Willie-driven exposé and the stories that we're oh-so-regretfully having to file just to keep up.

It's such a hot topic now that even the lawsuit-phobic Rita Dominick has to stand back and let news take its course. Eventually I'm sure she will sniff me out and find out the real story, then lay Wat Chenault's lawsuit in my in-basket as she gives me the pink slip. But, hell, we're having fun, aren't we?

While I wait for the clock to run out on L.D. Jones, I have time to give my favorite private eye a call. He's given me his cell number.

I can barely keep from giggling when he answers in what he must think is a Bogart voice:

"Sam Spadewell."

I explain to him that his services are no longer needed, that I have uncovered information that makes his sleuthing unnecessary. I haven't explained to Mr. Spadewell what it is exactly that I have suspected our favorite real-estate developer of doing in his leisure time. He's professional enough not to ask.

"Well," he says, "I guess that's that, then. I'll send you a bill."

I'm about to hang up when he says, "Don't you want to know what I found out? Might as well. You're payin' for it."

What the hell. I hoard free information all the time. I sure as hell want the crap I'm being dunned for. They're never going to let me put this one on my expense account.

And so he tells me.

He assures me he's got the stuff to prove it.

I compliment him on a job well done. He grunts and hangs up.

I was thinking about giving Wat Chenault a call, just to ease his mind enough so he won't be sending his knee-breakers after me in the near future. He's still going to sue our asses, but now maybe he won't think I have a personal hard-on for him.

Now, though, I think I'll just let this one ride a little bit.

CHAPTER NINETEEN

Saturday

That thing that has been rattling around in my brain has been driving me nuts. It's like when you try to think of some movie you used to love or an old girlfriend whose name has slipped just beyond your field of memory.

Sometimes it's best to just let it be. It will eventually come to you. My memory is like my Honda's semiworthless radio. It emits a lot of static, but once in a while it picks up a clear signal just when I least expect it.

And so it was that, lying in bed this morning, I had my epiphany.

Last night was only a two-beer evening at Penny Lane after work. This relatively healthful development along with the buzz I got from what I remembered has me up and at 'em a little after eight. I get a couple of Saturdays off per year, and this is one of them. So might as well make the most of it.

I go over to Peggy's, being very careful to knock and announce my presence. My mother offers me coffee. Andi asks me when it's going to be safe to work again, since her employer doesn't seem eager to pay her to stay home, death threat or no death threat. And then there's the school thing. If she can pass the three courses she's taking this semester, she will be perhaps one semester away from the Promised Land of graduation, although, with a baby on board, that semester might have to wait. Her professors have been understanding, but she's afraid of falling behind.

Awesome Dude is on one of his walkabouts. Peggy gives me a general idea of where he might be. I promise to drop by later for a more extensive visit. I wonder again about the effect of second-hand reefer smoke on fetuses.

"Be sure you have the safety on that thing," I tell her, pointing to the pistol on the kitchen counter.

"Of course I will," she says. "I'm not an idiot." As she says this, she reaches over and puts the safety on.

AFTER TWENTY MINUTES of scouring Oregon Hill, as I'm passing the river overlook for the second time, I spot him down below me. He seems to be taking in the view. I know that sometimes Awesome just needs to be by himself. I can relate.

He's sitting there on the ground, leaning forward with his head down. He gives a grunt and jerks up when I approach. I think I woke him up.

"Dude," he says. "Don't be sneaking up on me like that."

At least Awesome, unlike Peggy, is not armed. I apologize for interrupting his solitude.

I settle down beside him, and we both watch the James flow by for a couple of minutes. Some kayakers far below us are risking their lives for no good reason.

"Do you remember when you told me about the guy you saw, the night the Jonas girl was killed?"

It's been two weeks since he told me about it. Two weeks is a very long time for Awesome Dude's skittery memory. I try to bring him up to speed.

Finally he and I are, if not on the same page, at least in the same book.

"Oh, yeah," he says. "That girl down at the beach. Yeah. You didn't tell anybody about that, did you? Still feel bad about not saying nothing."

I ask him again about what he told me.

"There was a sound you said you heard there."

He doesn't seem to remember that.

"Was it like this?"

The sound works on him like an electric jolt.

"Shit! Yeah, damn! That was it. That was it. That's what I heard."

ON THE WAY back to my car, I call L.D. Jones's home number. I tell him why he and his troops ought to try really hard to reincarcerate Ronnie Sax. He understandably wants a little more information. I give it to him. After he curses me for doing what I promised I would, telling our readers about the latest communication with the killer, we eventually settle into a conversation modulated enough that I don't have to hold the phone three inches from my ear.

"That's sketchy as hell," he says. I further explain why my alternative theory about the Tweety Bird killings went south with the discovery of the quite alive-and-well Leigh Adkins.

I know the police have been turning Greater Richmond upside down, trying to find the bastard who's doing this, and nothing's turned up. Now they'll be back looking for Sax. Nobody at his apartment complex had set eyes on him as of last night.

"It was all your bullshit that made us release him in the first place," Jones says. "You and that damn Marcus Green and your wife."

I concede that this is true. My heart is heavy. I always try to be the dispassionate observer. I wonder if my genuine dislike for Wat Chenault has clouded my objectivity.

I apologize to the chief. He seems taken aback, having never heard me apologize before.

"Well," he says, "don't kill yourself over it. We're on this."

I truly hope they are. I have never wanted to see anybody fry as much as I do Ronnie Sax right now.

When I get back to my car, there's a ticket there. I never saw the no-parking sign. I doubt if L.D. Jones is going to fix this one for me.

AFTER A QUICK breakfast at Joe's, I call Cindy Peroni.

When I explain, in broad terms, what I want to do, she says she was afraid I was calling with some half-ass excuse for reneging on our date tonight. I assure her that a case of Ebola couldn't keep me away.

"That's comforting, in an insane kind of way."

"I really need to talk to her. I thought you might be able to break the ice."

Cindy sighs.

"I have a hair appointment at two. Let me see what I can do."

I give her her script.

"You want me to threaten her?"

"I just want you to tell her how it is."

Cindy calls back fifteen minutes later.

"OK. I told her what you said. I think it scared her. We can meet her at her house in an hour."

WE ARRIVE AT Mary Kate Brown's house at eleven forty-five. At first I don't think she's going to answer the door. Finally, though, it opens.

Ronnie Sax's sister looks like she hasn't been sleeping well. What I'm going to tell her isn't going to cure her insomnia. I really don't give a shit, at this point.

"You said some bad things to me," she says, casting an accusing look at Cindy. I'm thinking this friendship is on life support.

"She was just passing it on," I tell Ms. Brown. "She just told you what I told her to say. And, yes, I do think you're about this close to some big-time obstruction of justice."

She shakes her head.

"All right. What do you want to know?"

I explain about having found a witness who will swear he heard a camera whirr in the near aftermath of Kellie Jonas's murder down by the river. I oversell Awesome Dude's reliability as a witness. I explain my suspicions about the disappearance of Wat Chenault's one-time underage sex toy and how those suspicions were put to rest only yesterday.

"There isn't much else to think," I tell her in conclusion, "other than that the cops had the right guy all along."

She reaches for coffee. She hasn't offered us any. Her hand shakes.

"So why don't you go to the police?"

I explain that I have, and that they soon will be tearing our fair city apart brick by historic brick looking for her brother, but that she could help a lot by telling me just what parts of that bullshit story about Ronnie Sax's alibi the night of the last murder don't jibe with the hard, cold truth.

Yes, I could have passed this on to L.D. Jones. Part of me, though, wants to do it myself. Call me an egotistical bastard, but I've been chasing this story in circles, and I want some resolution. Plus I do have a little credibility with Mary Kate Kusack Brown. Just the fact that I'm not the police might help.

"OK," she says. "Ronnie got here a little later than I said, maybe eight thirty. But he didn't leave. I told the truth about that part."

I note that the detectives say the body was dumped down at the train station around nine thirty, based on when the now-unemployed night security guy went over to Havana 59 for his free drinks.

Ms. Brown nods her head. At first she doesn't offer any enlightenment. I wait.

Finally she gets up and starts pacing.

"I knew it," she says. "I knew it was going to be trouble. Ronnie, he isn't really a bad man. But he's easily led."

She doesn't elucidate. Finally, I ask.

"Led by who?"

She sits down again.

"Mr. Black," she says, "let me tell you about my brother."

I start to tell her that I know quite a bit about her brother already.

She stops me.

"No. My other brother."

CHAPTER TWENTY

"Are you sure you're doing the right thing?"

I appreciate Cindy's concern. And no, I'm not sure I'm doing either the right or the smart thing. But what Ronnie Sax's sister has told me makes me relatively certain that I finally know what the hell I'm doing. Better late than never.

I drop Cindy off at her house and thank her again for interceding with Mary Kate.

"It's no big deal," she says. "She must not have been that good of a friend anyhow. I can't believe she wasn't truthful with me."

I note that people will go a long way to protect their families, further than they should. Then I promise that I'll be back to pick her up at seven.

"You better be," she says. "I'm not wasting a hundred bucks on a hair appointment for nothing."

I STOP BY the Prestwould. Clara Westbrook meets me in the lobby, dressed to the nines and headed out. I hope, but doubt, that I will be so well turned-out if I ever hit eighty.

"Do you all know anything else about that monster?" she asks me.

I tell her that I hope to have news soon.

"Well, I certainly hope so," she says. "If the police don't catch him soon, I'm going to have to go down to Green Top and buy a gun. A girl's got to have some protection."

UP ON THE sixth floor, I make a sandwich and ponder my next move. I could call the cops, or I could go down to the Bottom by myself and see if Ronnie Sax's sister told the truth. Custalow would want to come along, but he's out on a deep-sea fishing excursion today with R.P. McGonnigal and a couple of other guys. I might be there myself if I liked puking and the risk of drowning a little more than I do.

What Mary Kate told me makes me think it'll be OK to just make a run to the building and check it out. Then if there's nobody there, I'll give L.D. Jones a call and make his day.

It's a beautiful Saturday afternoon. I catch the University of Virginia football game on the radio as I head east. The Wahoos are winning, but it's early.

Back when Richmond was riding high, all these warehouse buildings down along the James were hubs of commerce, built along the same stretch of river where, a few generations earlier, Africans disembarked at the end of one nightmare and the beginning of another. But that was before my time. By the time I was growing up, this was all a dead zone, enormous brick buildings waiting to be torn down.

Richmond is lucky, though. It didn't become a southern boomtown where the developers tore everything down. Around here, we'd rather sit and talk about the old days while we watch places like Tobacco Row eventually crumble into the river of their own volition.

Except this time they didn't. These buildings were made pretty well, I guess, not like the half-ass stuff that gets thrown together today. (Yeah, I pine for the old shit, too. So shoot me.) Eventually somebody needed more apartment space, and when developers started turning some of the warehouse buildings into apartments, the young hipsters were all over it, along with creeps like Ronnie Sax.

The building I'm looking for is one that hasn't made the transition yet from rat motel to luxury apartments. It'll come eventually, I'm sure, although, looking at the place, I wonder how.

I recheck the directions. Yeah, this is it. It's down near where the street alongside the river dead-ends. This is where Mary Kate said I could find Cordell Kusack. She begged me not to tell him who gave me his address. He apparently does not take well to betrayal.

Actually it isn't exactly an address. It's just a building waiting for better days. Apparently Mr. Kusack has been homesteading.

I am not, evidence to the contrary, a complete idiot. I call L.D. Jones's number and am told he's at a Virginia Union football game. When I tell his aide what I'm calling about, she's obviously been told that, for once, I'm at the top of the priority list. She gives me the chief's cell number. I reach L.D. Over all the stadium noise, I tell him to meet me at a grocery store parking lot not a mile from Kusack's alleged abode. I tell him to bring lots of armed folks with him. I could have told him the address, but I thought maybe it would be good if the cops didn't descend on the hideout like the cavalry, with sirens wailing and lights blazing. It seemed like a good idea at the time.

Mary Kate hasn't been here, but Ronnie has told her about it. Like her, he's sworn to secrecy by his big brother. He told his sister that there is a panel of plywood covering an opening on the side of the building facing the river. I sit in my car for maybe two minutes, looking for anything resembling life. The building is four stories high. About half the windows have been knocked out. I'm well beyond the next occupied space, maybe half a mile east of Ronnie Sax's apartment. The river is big down here. It's reflecting gold as the afternoon light hits it. You wouldn't willingly swim in it, but it is pretty to look at. Across the way, somebody desperate for food is fishing for carp or catfish. It's so peaceful I'd like to take a nap with the sun beaming in through my cracked windshield.

I start the car, ready to make a U-turn back to the grocery store where Richmond's finest soon will be converging like ants at a picnic.

"What the fuck do you want?"

I almost crap my pants. Whoever has what feels like a gun pressed against the back of my head came out of nowhere.

He repeats the question, with a little more enthusiasm and a rap upside my head with his free hand. I do a quick assessment and realize that I am at least 200 yards from other human beings. The guy with the cane pole across the river is probably the closest thing to help I could hope to rouse by screaming. I can't believe it. It's two o'clock on a Saturday afternoon in the middle of a decent-sized city, and I am alone, except for the guy with what I am now sure is a big-ass gun.

I start to explain that I'm just a guy out for a drive, enjoying the scenery.

He laughs, more or less, then reaches in, cuts the ignition and takes my keys.

"Yeah, I bet you are. I bet there's no chance you're that nosy-ass reporter my sister told me scared her into telling him about me. Yeah, no chance at all."

I guess that, for Mary Kate, blood turned out to be thicker than my promise not to drag her into this if her older brother turned out to be the monster I suspected he was. Or maybe she was just scared. Either way, I'm fucked.

Before I can deny my identity, he clips me pretty good with the gun.

"C'm'ere, asshole," I hear him tell somebody else. "Help me with these cuffs."

I hear the rear right-side door open. As I feel my hands being pulled behind me, I get a glimpse of my assailant's partner in the rearview mirror.

"Imagine meeting you here," I say as Ronnie Sax snaps the handcuffs behind me.

Ronnie gives that wheezy little laugh, which in some ways is scarier than his big brother and his big pistol.

They manage to get me out of the seat and over to the passenger's side, damn near separating my shoulder in the process. Ronnie hops back into the backseat and Cord Kusack gets behind the wheel.

He is able to maneuver the car down the side of the hill and into the small space between the warehouse and the river. I wonder if the guy across the way will notice and call the cops. When I glance over there, he looks like he's napping in his Kmart lawn chair.

I turn and get my first good look at Cord Kusack. What I see does not inspire confidence. While brother, Ronnie, mostly comes across as a perv who likes to mess with little girls, Cord is more along the lines of something out of the latest chainsaw movie.

For one thing, he's got to be eight inches taller than Ronnie, at least six seven, and I'd guess he goes about 280. He looks like a goddamn NFL defensive tackle, only scarier. His hair has either turned white or been bleached. It's standing more or less straight up. He has snakes tattooed on each side of his neck and a tuft of white soul patch on his chin that looks like somebody stuck a cotton ball there. His eyes are what get your attention, though. Or I guess you should say "eye."

The left one seems to be fixing me with a perpetual laser stare. The right one isn't there. Well, I mean, something's there, kind of milky and glassed over, floating there like a dead planet.

He must have noticed me staring.

"You like that?" he says as he orders Ronnie to pull nails out of the piece of plywood over the doorway and then pushes me inside. "Son of a bitch up at Lucasville did it with a razor blade. I'll show you how he did it a little later."

He laughs, his baritone and Ronnie's tenor harmonizing.

I can hear sirens in the distance, but they'll be waiting for me in that parking lot I can't get to. I tell my captors that I've called the police.

"Well," Cord says, "maybe you did. But I doubt it. If you did, we'll all go down together."

He laughs again, and they undo the handcuffs and throw me onto a floor that is partly decaying wood, partly dirt.

I could make a run for the opening where we came in, but Big Brother grabs me and puts a dog collar around my neck, then ties the rope connected to it to a post.

"There now," he says, "we'll have to gag you later, so nobody hears you, when we start going to work on you, but we won't do that just yet as long as you're good."

I promise to be very good. This is not turning out to be one of my ten favorite days. The sirens obviously aren't getting any closer.

"I bet you've got some questions," Kusack says, "you being a reporter and all."

MARY KATE HAS told me some of it. How Cord always had Ronnie in his hip pocket when they were single-parent latchkey kids, growing up in some dog-ass mill town in Ohio. How Cord and Ronnie got in trouble, with Cord always leading the way, when they were boys. Fires. Tortured animals. Terrorizing other kids. The usual psychopath-in-training stuff.

"Ronnie didn't want to be bad," she said, back in her living room an hour and a few light-years ago. "But Cord wouldn't let him alone. He made him do . . . stuff . . . and then threatened to tell everybody afterward if he didn't obey. He was so much bigger than us."

I didn't get into the "stuff" part, but I had the very strong impression that Mary Kate was forced to do "stuff" with her older brother, too.

"You don't understand," she said. "He has this way of making you do things. Not even physical. Well, not just physical. It was like he was inside our heads."

Mary Kate and then Ronnie somehow managed to get out of there and be pretty good students. They eventually went off to college, her to Ohio University and him to Virginia Commonwealth. She eventually transferred down here, too. Around the time Mary Kate left for Ohio U., Cord was arrested for a couple of rapes in his hometown. He had a record already, as a juvenile. Ronnie did, too, but compared with his brother, his transgressions were kids' stuff. I'm thinking VCU wasn't doing a lot of background checks on incoming freshmen.

The judge had dealt with Cord before, more than once. He knew a train wreck when he saw one, and he sentenced Cordell Kusack to twenty years, the most he could give him under state guidelines. Both girls were afraid to identify him on the witness stand, and the court had to settle for the testimony of a convenience-store clerk who saw him pull one of the girls into his car.

Cord managed to get more time added on while he was locked up. Looking at the son of a bitch now, I wonder what moron parole board ever saw redemption in this asshole.

"My mother had lost track of him," Mary Kate went on. "She said he just stopped writing. And, well, Ronnie and I, we didn't get back home much. Too many, you know, bad memories."

But Cord did get out, back in 2008. He showed up in Richmond in 2009.

"We never knew what he did after he got out, but when he got here and found Ronnie, it was like nothing ever changed. And the fact that Ronnie was, like, hanging around with models and all must have just played into Cord's hands.

"I never knew what they were doing, but I knew it wasn't good. But I didn't know, I swear."

The night of September 11, when Ronnie came to her house, she could tell something was wrong.

"He was all jittery, and then the next day I heard about that girl. And then they made Ronnie a suspect."

Mary Kate said she saw her older brother once after he moved to Richmond, and that he made it clear that she was never to tell anyone he was here. He'd busted parole in Ohio and done God knows what in his first year of freedom.

"I was scared," she said. "He can make you so scared you'll wet your pants."

Apparently he could make you scared enough to call him and tell him that a nosy-ass newspaper reporter was on his trail.

And so the best I could glean from today's little chat, Cordell Kusack, rapist, murderer and who knows what else, has been living incognito in our fair city for four years now. It makes you wonder who else is out there under the radar.

KUSACK, GOING UNDER the premise that dead men tell no tales, brings me up to speed on his more recent activities.

While he has me tied to the post, just for fun, he tases me. I've passed two kidney stones in my time, and this hurt worse. He gagged me first, so as not to disturb the neighbors.

"Just a preview of coming attractions," he says. I hear Ronnie snickering.

"We've been having fun, shithead and me," big brother says.

He sued the state of Ohio for letting one of his playmates have access to the razor with which Cordell Kusack's right eye was ruined. He won, somehow. Good thing he didn't try that crap in Virginia. So he's been drawing on that tidy sum for the last five years "plus my disability pay. Uncle Sam's been kind. And Little Ronnie's been helping out, right, Bro?"

He transferred the money to a joint bank account with Ronnie and has been drawing off of it. He's been off the grid since then.

"Had to move a couple of times, but this place looks like it'll do for a long time to come. We don't get too many visitors, though. Just the girls."

There are cloths over the windows, blacking out everything inside, but somehow we have a little bit of light. I'm just starting to wonder where it's coming from when Cord says, "Here, let me show you what I've done with the place."

Suddenly the far side of the room, which had been dark as a coal mine, is lit up like midday. I wish it hadn't been.

There, in living color on the brick interior wall, are the girls. I recognize them. Kelli Jonas. Chanelle Williams. Lorrie Estrada. And little Jessica Caldwell. None of them are dead yet in the first set of photographs, blown up to about three feet by four, which makes it all the more horrible. They all have arrived at a point at which death would be a mercy. Ronnie Sax's masterpiece: gagged and already put through hell, their eyes all say, "Kill me." I am afraid I'll throw up in my gag and choke to death.

"Ronnie does good work, don't you think?" my captor asks. He raises the Taser again, and I nod as emphatically as I can.

He explains how they managed to lure them all into this hellhole with drugs or force or both, and then scattered their bodies around town.

It apparently was quite the game for the Kusack boys, leaving the remains at well-known places around the city.

Kusack laughs, relating how easy it was to lure the women to dark, helpless places.

"They are so gullible," he says. "And I appreciate that. I really do."

Kusack is working off a generator and batteries here. Not all the comforts of home, but enough.

He learned about tattooing inside and then outside prison. He thought he might want to do that for a living. Richmond, to the anguish of the West End bluebloods, is America's tattoo capital. Go figure.

"But with the lawsuit money, well, I decided it'd be more fun to pursue my life's passion, make my masterpiece as it were."

He tells me about a couple of "practice sessions" he enlisted Ronnie in, where prostitutes suddenly disappeared and nobody really gave a shit.

I do have a vague recollection of a couple of hookers going missing, back when I was still covering the crooks in the General Assembly instead of the street variety.

"And then we got serious."

Kusack had been in town for nearly three years when he and Ronnie made their first grab.

"I wanted to leave a signature," he says, "so people wouldn't think this was some kind of mindless killing. I wanted it to have meaning."

They tattooed the girls here. Ronnie proudly adds that the silver dollars in the girls' clothing was his idea.

"Just a little calling card," big brother says. "After the second one, I wondered if the cops would even figure it out. They finally did. Do you know what a thrill it is, Mr. Reporter, to have a whole town scared shitless?"

Well I know what it feels like to be on the other end of that emotion.

I wonder, though, how this is going to work. Even after they kill me, the whole police force and whatever help they can bring in from outside is going to be looking for Ronnie Sax. Right now a large chunk of Saturday's crew must be a mile away. From where I'm standing, things don't look so good for Ronnie. I wonder if he's smart enough to know that.

"The key," Kusack says, "is to do one every six months, then lie low, just kind of letting the suspense build. Sometimes, though, it's hard to wait. Well, you'll provide us with a little entertainment in the meantime."

He knows his sister told me where he was. He doesn't know that Cindy Peroni shares that secret. For Cindy's sake, he's not going to find that out from me, no matter what.

He seems especially proud of the way he got Ronnie out of jail. He's been staying indoors most of the daylight hours and then using Ronnie's car at night, in addition to those throwaway cell phones, to convince our boys in blue, through me, that Ronnie Sax couldn't possibly have committed those terrible crimes.

He says he wore sunglasses so as not to spook the 7-Eleven clerks and other citizens.

"Ronnie knew I'd get him out," he says. "Hey, we're family. Can't let my little brother take the rap, can I?"

I'm thinking that Kusack's motives, humanitarian that he is, might not be quite that pure. Even if, as Cord says, Ronnie had sworn to forever hide his brother's identity, forever is a long time, especially if you're looking at a chemically induced dirt nap down at the prison where they put people like Ronnie out of our misery. Ronnie is capable of singing like a goddamn Tweety Bird. I think his brother and I both know that.

If I were Ronnie Sax, I wouldn't be buying any green bananas.

But you'll have to excuse me if Ronnie's health isn't my primary concern right now.

CHAPTER TWENTY-ONE

I come to. My first thought is that I'm going to be breaking yet another date with the lovely Cindy Peroni. My second thought is that I could definitely use a Camel and a Miller. And then the pain hits me.

Before they did the tattoo, the brothers dragged me over to a chair in the back of the room and tied me to it, my arms behind me and my ankles strapped to the legs. I was advised by Cordell Kusack to "shut the fuck up and hold still." It was as good a bit of advice as I was going to get under the circumstances. It hurt like a bitch when I thrashed around, which was hard not to do when he went to work on me with the needle. This was my first tattoo. I hope it's my last. It definitely was not on my bucket list. The bucket, by the way, seems well placed for that final kick right now.

The whole procedure took maybe twenty minutes but felt like a lot more.

"That way," Kusack says, "they won't have to wonder who did this to you."

"This," I understand, is going to be a lot more than a tattoo. There is a knife lying on the table not ten feet away. Kusack sees me looking at it.

"Not yet," he says. When he smiles, two gold teeth shine in the upper part of his mouth. Where they're positioned, they look like fangs. "Part of the fun is the anticipation. Not your fun, you understand. Me and Ronnie, we always have fun before the end, although you might not be as much fun as those girls were. But you've had about all the fun you're going to have, asshole."

I don't know what was on the rag he used to put me under. I just remember feeling like I was going to suffocate, and then nothing.

NOW WAKING UP, I get past this burning pain and try to focus. My ankle is on fire. I look down, and there it is, all bright and shiny and bruised. Tweety Bird.

Looking around the room, the only life form I see in the dim light is Ronnie Sax. He's sitting in an easy chair that looks like it came off a trash heap. He's reading what looks like an illustrated comic book, although closer examination reveals it to be one that could only be sold at the local fuck-book emporium. He seems to be reading it with one hand.

I make as much noise as I can through the gag. Ronnie puts his porn down and walks over.

"Whatta you want?"

He's trying to be Mr. Tough Guy, disremembering that we used to work together and I know what a putz he is. He's still Ronnie Sax, a wheezy little guy who's mostly a threat to those smaller than himself.

"If I take the gag off," he says, "you gotta promise not to yell, or I'll have to hurt you."

He puts his right hand on the Taser. Compared with what big brother is planning, Ronnie's threats aren't adding to my anxiety.

He tells me that his brother has gone out.

"He's got to get some money from the ATM," Ronnie says. "He told me we're probably going to have to get out of town, maybe go to Canada for a while."

I thank him for removing the gag. And then I start in. They always said, on Oregon Hill, that I could sell refrigerators to the Eskimos. A lot is riding on my still having the gift of gab.

"So you and Cordell are gonna skip town."

Nothing from Ronnie.

"You know, Cordell seems like a smart guy. Know what I'm betting?"

He's still not talking to me, but he stops what he's doing. I know he's listening.

"I'm betting that Cordell has already figured that he can travel faster alone . . ."

"Shut up."

"Well," I continue, keeping my voice just loud enough that he can hear me without doing something that'll encourage him to silence me again, "here's the thing. If Cord is really dotting the I's and crossing the T's, he won't want anybody around who can get caught and maybe tell the police who's really responsible for all this."

Ronnie turns toward me.

"He knows I'd never tell on him. I never did. Not to Momma or anybody."

"But, let's just say, for the sake of argument, that he was to come back here, do whatever he's planning to do to me. Then wouldn't it be a lot easier just to shoot you and leave you lying here dead on the floor? Maybe make it look like a suicide?"

"I'm gonna put that gag back in your mouth. You're talking bullshit, man."

But he doesn't put the gag back.

I take a deep breath.

"And maybe he'll want to get rid of your sister. She's already told me about Cord. Sure she called and warned him, but who knows when she might get scared into talking to the cops?"

"Mary Kate? He wouldn't hurt Mary Kate."

I let that one hang while Ronnie Sax mulls it over in his feeble mind, maybe trying to drown out that little voice I've planted there.

He comes back over, his face red and furious in the light.

"No! Cord wouldn't do that. He said if we did what he said, nothing bad would happen."

"But you got caught. And Mary Kate talked."

He gets right in my face. There is actual spittle on his chin.

It is my chance, maybe my only one. Another thing I was known for on the Hill, growing up, was my hard head. I did that thing a couple of times in fights, where you walk up to some guy who's ready to tear you apart, and you just head-bump him. Hard. I don't know why some people can do this and some can't. Maybe I have an overload of calcium. Maybe my family is just naturally thickskulled. Look at Peggy.

When Ronnie's maybe six inches away, I spring out of the chair with all the energy I have left, more or less throwing myself at the idiot.

Ronnie drops like he's been shot. I have knocked out the softheaded son of a bitch. For how long, I don't know, but it's a break, and I'm desperately in need of one.

I see the knife shining in the dim light. I manage to wrestle that chair across the room. I back up to the knife, praying that Ronnie Sax is out for at least the next twenty minutes.

I can feel the knife cutting into my skin behind me as I wedge it against the side of the table, trying to get in just the right position to saw the rope holding my hands in place. It feels like I'm taking as much skin as rope, but finally, after maybe ten minutes, I feel the rope loosen a little bit, then a little more, until I can get one hand out and then the other.

I reach down, still trying to get some feeling back in my hands, and undo the straps holding my ankles. My right wrist is kind of a mess. I look like a bungled suicide attempt and my ankle's on fire from the involuntary tattoo. But who gives a damn? I'm free. I have a fighting chance. More than one editor has called me a hard-headed bastard. Well, you use what you've got.

And that's when I hear footsteps outside. As far as I can tell, there's only one way out of this hellhole, the window frames being some kind of metal, and it sounds like either Cordell Kusack or a police posse come to rescue me is outside right now. The way my luck's been going lately, I'm not betting on the posse.

And so I retreat back into the dark. Beyond the light, this warehouse is black as the pits of hell. It must go back a couple of hundred feet. I go about halfway back to hide until I find out who's out there.

And, of course, it's Kusack. He looks a little wild-eyed, even by his standards.

"What the fuck?" he says when he sees his brother lying on the floor, still in la-la land.

He talks to him like he thinks Ronnie can hear him.

"Goddammit, man. I leave you to do one thing, one thing, and you fuck it up."

He sounds more sad than angry.

"Well, this just makes it a little easier."

He's probably thirty yards away, and I can just make out the pistol in his hand. I can barely hear him when he says it: "Bye-bye, Bro."

The gunfire makes me jump. He shoots into Ronnie Sax's unconscious body five times. I can see what is now a corpse jump from the impact.

Kusack looks around the room, looking first at the door and then staring into the darkness, right at me although he can't possibly see me from where he is.

He reaches around behind his head and rubs his neck.

"Well," he says, raising his voice as if he is expecting someone else to hear him, "that door hadn't been touched since I left, and there ain't but one way out of here.

"So," he says, saying it like he's playing a game with a kid, "come out, come out, wherever you are."

What a dumbass I am. Ronnie had a pistol on him, too, and I didn't take it off him. In my panic, I didn't even think to grab the knife. Well you can't think of everything.

So here comes a six-foot-seven nightmare with a gun. It just doesn't seem fair. I'd like to claim my Second Amendment rights to have some heat, but it's a little late for that. Glenn Walker, the present husband of my first wife, once gave me a pistol when it appeared I might need one. I think I turned it in to the cops at one of those drives to cut down on the city's firepower. Like that ever works.

He steps and walks back to a low table by one of the windows and picks up a flashlight. Shit.

"Well," he says, calm as can be, "I've taken care of two of my problems now. Let's see if we can make it three for three."

Now he's making his way toward me, a step at a time, the gun in his right hand, waving the flashlight from side to side with his left. I figure he can see maybe twenty feet away. From where I stand, pushed against a wall, he's a monster silhouette, lurching toward me like an extra in some zombie movie.

He's maybe twice that distance when I make my move. There really isn't much choice.

The feeling is more or less back in my legs, but I am still no threat to win the forty-yard dash. I don't remember bumping into anything on the way back here and hope my memory is correct.

I have no intention of trying to fight Cordell Kusack. I'm a welterweight and he's definitely a heavyweight. My hope is to somehow dash past him and get to that plywood door before he shoots my ass.

He must see me just before I draw even with him. As he raises his left arm, I collide with him. The flashlight goes flying. Kusack lets out a roar.

I'm still in the dark when I hear that first shot, echoing, and half-deafening me. He's wide of the mark, but I don't have much of a head start. When I burst into the lighted part where Kusack has been more or less living, it seems impossible that I could get that makeshift door open and get out before he brings me down.

I see the knife, still lying there with my blood on it. I dive for it and crawl behind the chair where I was sitting. Kusack fires a shot into the chair, and my luck holds out again.

There is only one option. Before he can try again, I rush him. Maybe it surprises him a little. I don't know. All I know is that when I get to point-blank range, I go for his eye. The good one. The first time I'm a little wide of the mark, but so is his second shot. I only leave a gash along the side of his head. The next time, while he's a bit distracted with the blood and all, I hit dead center. I try to drive that damn blade all the way through. I've never killed anyone before. It feels good, standing there with Ronnie Sax's blood sticking to my feet.

He squeals like a stuck pig, falling to the floor with the knife still sticking out of the socket of what was his only good eye. I'm still not sure he won't fight through the pain, and he hasn't let go of the gun that's still in his twitching right hand.

I run. I tear that plywood door from its makeshift hinges and scurry outside, free at last. It's dark. My car is between my escape hatch and the river, but I don't know where the keys are, probably on either the dead body of Ronnie Sax or the still live one of his brother. It occurs to me that he might have used my car to make a trip to Mary Kate's house.

I reach into my pocket. Amazingly, my cell phone is still there. I run up the same ramp we came down a few hours earlier and don't stop until I'm on the street, a good hundred yards away from the place that I thought a short while ago would be my last stop on this planet.

I call 9-1-1 and give them as good a description as I can of my location. The dispatcher is calm and cool. Half the police force has been looking for me. I can hear the sirens already. I tell her to tell them to hurry.

And then I call Cindy Peroni and tell her it looks like she's going to have to take another rain check.

CHAPTER TWENTY-TWO

The cops are there in less than two minutes. I'm hiding in the bushes, keeping one eye on the warehouse building where I left Cordell Kusack.

When I hear the sirens and see the blue lights approaching, I jump out and wave the first one down. And who should it be but Gillespie, my doughnut-devouring frenemy of many years.

"I should have known," he says. "If there's shit stirred up, you're bound to be there with a stick in your hand."

I explain, as quickly and succinctly as I can, what has happened. When I tell him and the other cops—there are three cars now, with more coming—that I think the Tweety Bird Killer is inside the warehouse building in front of them, it gets their attention. I also give them an address on the North Side where I think they might find a female body.

They wait another ten minutes before coming up with a plan of action, which consists of cordoning off the area and telling Cordell Kusack, via bullhorn, to come out with his hands up.

Then the SWAT guys take positions on both sides of the building. I've assured them that there is only one way in or out, but they have to see for themselves.

At last they make their move. They throw one of those flash-bang grenades inside and go tearing in right after it.

I want to tell them that the flash part won't have much of an impact on the now-blind if not dead Cordell Kusack, but I don't want to butt in. I'm watching from a hundred yards away, which is as close as they'll let me come. They're in there for what seems like a long time, and I don't hear gunfire.

I call Sally Velez and tell her she's going to have to remake A1, and why. I tell her I'll try to get there within a couple of hours. I take a few pictures with my iPhone camera of cops picking their noses. Gillespie tells me to stop. I tell him to go fuck himself.

By this time, half the town seems to be here. L.D. Jones has been in attendance since he left the football game in the third quarter. He's still wearing his Virginia Union sweatshirt. A large contingent of Shockoe Bottom residents and revelers has made its way to the edge of the yellow police tape, sensing free entertainment.

Cindy is there maybe twenty minutes after I called. She gives me a venti-size hug and then gives me hell for trying to go it alone. I try to explain that I didn't really plan to be abducted by maniacs. It just worked out that way.

When she stops yelling for a second or two, I lean down and give her a kiss and thank her for caring. She kisses me back.

Meanwhile the cops seem a bit confused. I learn, through eavesdropping and pestering, that Cordell Kusack is not inside the warehouse. Yes, they checked all over, with floodlights on. There apparently was no way to get from the first floor to the ones above, and the only life form they found on the first floor was the bullet-riddled body of Ronnie Sax, whose brother definitely was not his keeper.

"Looks like a damned slaughterhouse in there," I hear one cop say.

One of the detectives, a guy I've known since my first gig on the night cops beat, asks me if I'm sure it wasn't me who shot Sax. I told him that I'd done all my damage with a knife.

"Didn't see no knife," the detective says. I tell him Kusack might still be wearing it.

I ask him if I get a reward. He tells me not to go anywhere. I tell him I wouldn't dream of it.

When the cops aren't looking, I manage to slip inside the tape and fall in step with Gillespie. I tell Cindy I'll be right back. Gillespie starts to tell me to get the hell out of there. I tell him I've got too much invested in this to go back now, that if he wants to tase me, it won't be the first time today. Hell, if he wants to shoot at me, he won't break a cherry there, either, as long as he doesn't hit anything. He shrugs and tries to ignore me. With a couple of pints of Cordell Kusack's blood on me, maybe he thinks I've earned the right to be here.

It's kind of a madhouse near and inside that plywood door. An ambulance has arrived to take Ronnie Sax's body away. L.D. Jones is shaking his head.

I'm out on the edge of the clusterfuck, close to the river. There's a concrete pier jutting out into the James, and I step out there to enjoy my first Camel of the evening. My hands are shaking a little. I'm sure a little nicotine will knock that right up.

With all the hubbub, I don't guess anybody else hears the voice. I look around and finally locate the speaker. It's the same old guy that's been across the river, probably all day, hoping for a catfish.

I move as close to the edge of the pier as I can, and I finally make out what he's saying.

"He went thataway," the man is saying. "He went downstream."

That's when I look down and see Cordell Kusack's gun, lying five feet away from me on the concrete. Beside it is the knife. When the first cop sees what's stuck to it, he turns to one side before he throws up.

CHAPTER TWENTY-THREE

Monday

I have some serious comp time coming.

I feel within my rights to count Saturday as a workday, since I spent a large part of it tied up in a Shockoe Bottom warehouse, waiting to be tortured to death for being a nosy-ass reporter. And I did get back to the office in time to write a stop-the-presses piece for Sunday's paper. They never found my car keys, but L.D. Jones was so thrilled at the prospect of informing the city that it was shy a psychopath or two that he gave me a ride in his own, personal car.

I'm counting yesterday as an eight-hour day, too. They let me kill a few trees explaining, as best I could, the whole sorry saga of the brothers Kusack and Sax. I doubt if it makes the parents of Kelli Jonas, Chanelle Williams, Lorrie Estrada and Jessica Caldwell feel a damn bit better, but the shrinks are always talking about closure, so maybe that's something.

The photo chief wanted to get a shot of my new, unwanted tattoo. After fighting it all the way up to Wheelie, I agreed. I hang people's dirty underwear on the public clothesline all the time. I guess I'm in no position to shun the spotlight. When I said something about "not pulling a Garbo," Sarah Goodnight asked me to translate that from old folks into English. The kids they send us these days.

They found the body of poor Mary Kate Kusack Brown, as I feared they would. She was apparently shot dead by her dear brother just inside her front door. Her daughters found the body when they got home from a sleepover.

Mary Kate and Ronnie seem to have been under the spell of their brother—a spell of pure evil. They thought they had escaped it, but it found them, and they were either too intimidated or too weak to resist. In Ronnie's case, it didn't help that he already had a sweet tooth for the kind of sexual misbehavior that can earn you a long sentence even if you don't kill anyone. Maybe big brother nurtured that particular kink when they were still kids. Who knows? And there's no one around to tell us—at least not right now.

Sunday and Monday are my usual days off, but today there's more to write. We're still trying to retrace Kusack's steps and figure out how this maniac was able to live off the grid for years while he's supposed to be a parolee up in Ohio. Turns out somebody up there had him marked as "presumed dead," probably because they were too damn lazy to track him down. Out of state, out of mind.

Wheelie said someone else could jump in and pick up the ball if I wanted some time off. I told him I'd give this story up when they tear it from my cold, dead, nicotine-stained hands.

FEAR HANGS OVER the newsroom today like cigarette smoke once did. Newsrooms are marginally healthier, but the business still needs a quintuple bypass, and we're having chest pains.

It turns out that the Friedman chain's vultures have been circling again. Sally Velez says two of their hired guns were around this weekend, kicking the tires. It was all hush-hush, but somebody got the mystery men's license plate number, and within a couple of hours everyone knew who they were. Never try to keep a secret from a journalist, especially if his or her livelihood is involved. That really inspires us.

"I hear they came into the newsroom of that paper they bought down in Carolina and told everybody to turn in their resignations, and they would decide who to keep," Enos Jackson said. "It took 'em about a week to clean house."

I worry about Enos. He's only here because of a deal I worked out three years ago with our now-late publisher. I doubt if that free pass has conveyed from James "Grubby" Grubbs to our new publisher. Enos doesn't know about the deal. No sense in worrying him now. Things could always be worse. One of the other state papers got bought by an investment group last year, whose only reason for existence was to turn a short-turn profit for their investors by buying distressed properties (newspapers) cheap, improving the bottom line by cutting expenses and selling high. Reporters and editors fall under the category of expenses. Within six months, half the newsroom was gone.

Speaking of our new publisher, Ms. "Call me Rita" Dominick phones down to request the honor of my presence. I don't know whether she's going to give me a raise or fire me for my role in besmirching the fine reputation of Wat Chenault. I ask her if we can meet at three, because I have to finish a story and then be out of the office for a bit for a very important meeting.

"Can't you cancel the interview?" she asks me.

I tell her that, if things go well, she will be glad I went to this particular meeting.

"I'd like a few more details."

"I can't give them to you right now. I'm sworn to secrecy."

She doesn't seem to exactly believe me. Trust is such a fragile thing.

She sighs. Clearly I exasperate her. I have that effect on publishers.

"Well," she says, "you'd better be here at three. Your presence might determine whether you still have a job."

Bullshit, I'm thinking. I've just given you the best story this rag's going to have all year. And by the time the big hand's on twelve and the little hand's at three, you're not going to have to worry about Wat Chenault.

I called him yesterday. I didn't tell him everything I knew, just dropped one name that I was sure would make him swallow his bile and make room for me in his busy, busy schedule.

WE MEET AT his office at one thirty. Sitting in the outer sanctum, I'm pretty sure I recognize one of the goons who accompanied us the day Wat took me for that ride around Richmond. I nod. He scowls.

Things are not going well for Top of the Bottom. The story I bequeathed to the *Scimitar*, the subsequent ones in our paper, and those pesky bones of former slaves that interested parties continue to dig up seem to have turned the tide against Chenault's project. Even the mayor, who had been acting like Wat's junior partner, is starting to back off. Reelection isn't that far away.

And so, between all that potential money flying out the window and Chenault's knowing that I went way out of my way to try to prove he was the Tweety Bird Killer, he has some legitimate reasons to hold a grudge.

I wait fifteen minutes. Finally Chenault's secretary ushers me in. The fat man's office wall does not disappoint. There's a deer head mounted on it. Beside that is a Confederate battle flag. Wat is sitting in his leather chair, smoking a cigar and glowering at me. He doesn't offer me a seat, but there are two chairs facing him, and the suit, who turns out to be his mouthpiece, is in the other one. I sit.

"What the hell do you want?" he asks.

"I think you know," I tell him. "I want you to drop the lawsuit."

The lawyer laughs. Chenault doesn't. He's obviously not told his hired boy the name I relayed to Wat yesterday, and what it means.

"I'll have your ass," the fat man says, setting the cigar down carefully on the lip of an ashtray.

I nod toward the lawyer.

"Tell him why you won't."

Chenault is silent.

When I start to speak, he holds up one pink palm.

"OK, OK, no sense in letting this get out of hand. I doubt you have enough, uh, information to cause me any serious harm."

He's fishing. I'm not biting.

The expression on the lawyer's face indicates he thinks he and Wat need to talk. He doesn't know yet why his client's boot heel isn't on my neck anymore.

"Look," I tell them, "I don't have time for this. I've got an important meeting at three."

I turn to the lawyer.

"I don't want to embarrass your client," I tell him, "and cost you a big fee, in addition to maybe sending his fat ass to Greensville for a few years, but you need to know some stuff, counselor."

Actually I don't really give a damn whether Wat Chenault goes to prison or not. I just want to break even on this one.

DESPITE HIS DUMBASS *nom de sleuth*, Sam Spadewell is not a complete idiot. At least he wasn't on this occasion.

You'd think Chenault would have learned something from the incident that cost him his political career, but old habits die hard.

It took Spadewell less than a week hanging out at the high-end place Wat was renting overlooking the river to come up with the photographs and audio.

The audio, from a wire Spadewell planted, was especially juicy. When I played a bit of it, the lawyer reached up and rubbed his temple, like he needed a Tylenol.

He was a gamer, though.

"That won't hold up in court," he said.

Of course it won't. But as I explained to him and my old buddy Wat, it wouldn't really have to. After the girl was confronted with the tape, in the flophouse where she and a couple of other runaways were staying, making a living any way they could, she was surprisingly compliant in explaining, gory chapter and verse, what she and "Mr. Walker" had been up to. Maybe she just wanted to do the right thing. Maybe it was Spadewell assuring her that she was going to face prostitution and drug charges if she didn't help us out.

I can tell the lawyer hates to ask the question:

"How old?"

"Fourteen."

"That's not possible," Chenault blurts out. "She swore to me she was seventeen . . ."

He stops, perhaps realizing that seventeen is not quite old enough for legal sticklers, either. Or maybe he can hear himself and knows how goddamn stupid he sounds.

"I wasn't hurting anybody," he says, almost whining. I want to slap him.

I'm not exactly on a moral pedestal here. I've arranged, through a woman Peachy Love knows in human services, to get this little girl lined up with the kind of help that might make it easier for her to find a life that doesn't include blowing fifty-eight-year-old pedophiles. A better man might have just gone to the cops (for the moment, L.D. Jones owes me a little attention) and sent Wat Chenault to a place where they might do to him what he had been doing to that girl.

But I'm not sure Chenault couldn't wiggle his way out of it, with his money and connections. And I want that lawsuit to disappear. I've also made it clear to Wat that if anything untoward happens to me in the next twenty years, there are people who will quickly tell the police who Suspect Number One is.

By the time I leave the fat man's office, we seem to be on the same page. I don't bother nodding at the goon on the way out.

THEY FOUND MOST of Cordell Kusack. Dead or alive, he washed up onshore at an island in the James a couple of miles downriver. By the time a couple of fishermen saw his body and called 9-1-1, the animals had had a go at him. I hope he wasn't dead yet when this happened, but you can't have everything.

I'm almost sorry it ended this way. This state is more trigger-happy than most when it comes to the ultimate penalty, and I wouldn't have minded Kusack being officially administered a smidgen of the pain he caused those girls. I wouldn't have minded watching.

This way, though, at least their parents can rest easy knowing that justice, weak consolation prize that it is, has been served without having the whole nightmare played out again in a courtroom.

How do I feel about driving a knife through another human being's eye socket? I've been in plenty of fights, when I was younger, but I had never done this kind of damage. With a knife, you have a lot more buy-in than you do with a gun. I won't get the sight, sound and feel of it out of my head anytime soon.

But regrets? Not a damn one.

RITA DOMINICK IS waiting for me. Sandy McCool seems to know that I'm five minutes late and seems concerned for my future employment. She doesn't say anything; I can just see it in her usually inscrutable face.

I wink at her and open the door to the publisher's office, walking in unannounced.

Dominick is on the phone and makes me wait a good five minutes more, probably just to show me who's boss.

"So," she says as she puts the phone down, "you finally made it back, I see."

I ask her if there's a problem.

"Problem? No, there's no problem. Maybe you think you're out of the woods because of that story you stumbled into."

She has some kind of ball in her hand, the kind you use to relieve stress, in lieu of throwing a paperweight at a reporter.

"Do you know how much Wat Chenault is going to sue us for? This lawsuit by itself could be enough to keep . . . well, to make us a lot less attractive."

"To the Friedmans, you mean?"

She glares at me.

"It's none of your business to who."

"Whom."

"You're correcting my goddamn grammar now?"

Well, I stop short of saying, "I should cut you some slack. You did come from advertising."

"You think I don't know who fed that story to the *Scimitar*? You think I don't have some connections? And if I know who tipped that rag off about Chenault, don't you think he's going to find out, too?"

I clear my throat and stand up. I've caught about enough shit for the time being.

"You asked me if I knew how much Wat Chenault was going to sue us for."

She stops ranting.

"What? Oh. That's what I think they call a rhetorical question."

I can hear the sarcasm dripping like a leaky faucet.

I wait a couple of seconds.

"Nevertheless I have an answer for you."

She looks puzzled.

"On how much he's going to sue us for. The answer is zero. He is not going to sue us for one fucking cent. At least he won't as long as I know what I know and don't tell anybody what I know. You know?"

She is smart enough to let me finish.

"If I'm still working here, Wat Chenault doesn't sue us for a penny. If I somehow become unemployed, this paper and Chenault are both up to their necks in shit."

She wants to know more, of course. I tell her she's on a need-to-know basis, and I've decided she doesn't need to know.

"Now," I tell her, "if you'll excuse me, I have a story to write."

She's still talking when I walk out, something about insubordination.

Lady, I want to tell her, I was insubordinating when you were still teething.

CHAPTER TWENTY-FOUR

Sunday, October 6

"Dude, can't we make this thing sit still?"

Awesome is having a little trouble finding his sea legs. Hell, he doesn't do that well with his land legs.

Maybe it wasn't the best idea in the world bringing him out here, but he's family now, and this is a family day. Well, family and a few friends. Peggy and Andi are here, of course. And Cindi and Custalow and R.P. McGonnigal, whose latest love interest, a guy with more money than he knows what to do with, is our captain.

And, of course, Les is here.

It's a big boat.

The water makes me think of Cordell Kusack, whose body might have made it out here to the Bay if it hadn't gotten snagged on that island in the James. Hopefully he's been roasting over a spit in hell for a few days.

Les would be pleased by our plan. He always said he wanted his ashes scattered over the Chesapeake. In the year and a half since his death, we have absently wondered from time to time how exactly we were going to do that. It wasn't Job One. Peggy seemed more than happy to keep what was left of the love of her life sitting in a jar on the mantel. She had few compunctions about telling a few miscreant husbands and boyfriends to hit the road, posthaste, but she kind of wanted to hang on to Les. We all did.

But then I happened to mention it one night when R.P., Andy Peroni, Abe, and I were playing poker. R.P.'s friend was there, sitting in.

I was talking about how hard it was going to be, logistically. I mean we couldn't just drop his ashes in the York River or some creek up in Annapolis and hope they found their way to the deep water. And none of us had a boat.

"Hell," R.P.'s partner said, "I've got a boat."

And so here we are, a mile or so offshore with Reedville fading into the haze behind us.

"I think this'll do," I tell the captain. Peggy nods.

We heard about a service that puts people's ashes into biodegradable boxes that will sink "in a minute or two" and not do any further violence to the Bay—in addition to avoiding the too-frequent occurrence of loved ones' ashes blowing back in the faces of the mourners. So I had Les's ashes transferred to one of those. We have it beside us on the boat.

Les deserved better than to be picked off with a high-powered rifle by a deranged killer who had it in for everybody on the 1964 Richmond Vees, his last stop in a pro baseball career that never got beyond Triple-A. But, like old Mick Jagger says, you can't always get what you want.

And so we're here to do right, the best way we know, by a man who always did right.

I pick up the box and ask if anyone has anything to say.

"Mom?"

"Damn," Peggy says, "I don't even go to church. If I start praying, we might get hit by lightning."

But I say a few words, about him being the best father I never had, and then Andi and Custalow join in. Awesome just says, "Dude. Sleep good." Finally, Peggy steps up.

"That's enough. We've wasted enough time out here, hauling your ashes, you old bastard."

I hug her. She and I drop the box off the side of the boat. Andi has brought along some rose petals. She sprinkles them in the water. I watch to make sure she doesn't get too close to the edge. The baby's making her kind of front heavy.

And we wait for the box to sink. And wait. And wait.

The captain is following it, very slowly, with his boat as it floats like a cork on the Chesapeake. I remember that, for some reason, Les's name is on the bottom of the box.

"We have to get it back in," I tell the captain. He shakes his head and points me to a net with a long handle, no doubt for hauling in rockfish. It'll do.

I reach over the side of the boat and, with Custalow holding me to keep me from falling in, I pull Les Hacker back out of the Bay.

We open the box and look down at Les's ashes in the container inside. We scratch our heads for a few minutes. Then I hear Peggy. At first I think she's crying, but I overestimate my mother's sentimentality.

"Oh, Les," she says as she doubles over with laughter, "you always were a good swimmer."

"Looks like he was headed for Bermuda," Custalow adds.

Soon we are all howling, even the captain. We expected tears today, but not this kind. And I know that Les would be laughing with us, if he could.

The captain has us half fill the box with water. We set it back in the Bay. In a couple of minutes, it finally starts its slow descent, sinking below a path of rose petals.

R.P. starts opening the beers. We could all use a little closure.